Her Dark Master

Risque Regencies, Volume 1

Jennifer August

Published by Jennifer August, 2021.

This is a work of fiction. Similarities to real people, places, or events are entirely coincidental.

HER DARK MASTER

First edition. February 7, 2021.

ISBN: 978-1940061047

Written by Jennifer August.

Also by Jennifer August

Masters of the Night
Bound By His Blood

Risque Regencies
Her Dark Master

Standalone
Strokes at Midnight
Knight of the Mist
His Lady Thief
Affair of Convenience

Watch for more at https://www.jenniferaugust.com/.

For those who believed in me, encouraged me, and always insisted I could. I miss you all. Mom, Dad, Big Bro.

Chapter One

VICTORIA ROSE ASHFORD sat primly in the front salon, watching through lowered lashes as her mother gushed over the once-again visiting Colonel Jameson. Though the man cut a debonair and trim figure, the heavy gray at his temples coupled with the wide blunt of his mustache reminded her more of a grandfather than pleasing suitor.

No, he was most unsuitable, regardless of her mother's rather forceful attempts to make a match. Mother made her desires – warnings? – quite clear, but Tori dismissed those as idle threats. Refusing proposals was not uncommon when a girl was still in her first few seasons. Why, her best friend Laurel Edison had turned down two suitors. She remained unmarried and the world did not grind to a halt.

"Miss Ashford, favor me with a turn at the pianoforte."

Stifling a sigh, Tori took a seat at the instrument, taking as much time as she dared to arrange her skirts, the music, the cushion beneath her. While she thought his high-handed manner came from his years of military experience, there always seemed to be something else just beneath the surface of his words. Something slithering and unwanted. Certainly beyond that, the man expected his every order to be obeyed as though she were a soldier in his command. Irksome man.

Obeying Matthew, however... Tori shivered at the delicious, though likely impossible, thought.

Colonel Jameson shifted in his chair and she knew he would chastise her and order her to play again. Rather than appear to bend to his brusqueness, Tori brought her fingers to the keys and played, deftly coaxing a tune from the pianoforte. Not her favorite activity, by far, but at least it precluded conversation with the Colonel. She cared little for his battlefield exploits or his stern command of the Indian people who fell beneath his jurisdiction. He was much too rigid for her tastes.

Polite applause followed the last strains of music and she stood, giving a light curtsy.

"You play splendidly, Miss Ashford."

"Thank you, Colonel." The mouthed platitude sounded forced and insincere to her ear, but he seemed to take no note of it.

Instead, he studied her intently and she wondered if it was her overactive imagination or if his gaze *did* linger at her breasts. Surely he would not commit such a breach of etiquette?

"Do you have any other talents, Miss Ashford? Singing? Poetry, mayhap?"

Tori cleared her throat and smiled at him. "No, I am afraid the pianoforte is my only real talent."

His mustache quivered alarmingly and his lips curled back. "I doubt that, my dear. It is my finding that young women such as yourself are remarkably talented in all sorts of areas. Once they receive proper instruction."

She blinked, positive she misheard. Misunderstood. Her secret writings must be affecting her more than she first believed if she was finding hidden meaning in the most innocent of comments.

"You are absolutely correct, Colonel," her mother said, moving to stand beside him. "Victoria has always been a quick study."

"Indeed?" the Colonel murmured, his shuttered gaze stalking her.

Tori shivered.

Her mother slipped her arm through his elbow. "Would you like another cup of tea, Colonel?"

Finally pulling his eyes away, he shook his head. "No thank you, Lady Ashford, I must be off. I trust I will find you both at the Harrington ball?"

"Yes, of course."

"And you, my dear, will you consent to allowing me a spot on your dance card?"

Tori slanted a discreetly pleading look at her mother, to no avail. Swallowing hard, she nodded. "As you wish."

His mustache quivered again and she caught the huff of air as he exhaled.

"Very good. Very good, indeed." The Colonel's eyes glinted. "Lady Ashford, if you run into our mutual friend Mr. Wolffe, would you be so good as to pass along my greetings?"

Tori glanced quizzically over at her mother's in-drawn breath, surprised to see two small lines bracketing her mouth. "I am quite certain I shall not see him again, Colonel."

"But just in case, please keep my words in mind." With a bow and a final intense stare, he was gone.

Tori did not even wait for the door to close behind him before dashing up the stairs, skirts high in hand.

"Victoria," her mother said sharply, stopping her at the top of the staircase.

She looked back. "Yes?"

"Come sit with me, please."

Tori slowly walked back down the stairs, studying her. Behind the green eyes they shared seemed to lurk a shadow, but she was not certain. Of late, she'd grown more assertive in her desire to see Tori wed. The friction between them over the subject reared frequently, but she knew deep down her mother only wished her happiness. Didn't she? While never the warmest of mothers, she'd never turned either of her children away when they needed her, took them on picnics when they were young, carefully orchestrated their growth into adults. Only in the last month had this odd chasm grown between them. An emotional whirlwind Tori could not decipher.

She sat on the sofa, hoping this was not going to be yet another lecture on the necessity of a good marriage. She already knew that. She also knew Corwin would be the absolute finest match she could make. *If* she could make it.

Given his total indifference to her, Tori feared a liaison between them would be an impossibility. However, she was not quite ready to give in. She still had time. She joined her brother Ryder and Matthew Corwin, Earl of Sussex once a month for shooting lessons. She lived for those days when she managed to make Matthew forget she was more than a child and less than his friend's sister. A pity they didn't occur more often.

"I have given you plenty of opportunity to secure your own future, have I not?"

Heart tightening, she stiffened. "What do you mean?"

A frown marred her mother's brow and she rubbed her fingers to her temple then shrugged. "You cannot have Corwin, Tori. You must leave that childhood dream behind and accept your future as a woman. A woman of status, married to a man with the wealth and means to care for you gloriously for the remainder of your years."

The words ripped at her and she ducked her head, refusing to allow any tears to fall. "I harbor no lost hope on Corwin, Mother, but neither do I wish for comfort over love."

"With security comes love, Victoria. The Colonel can offer you that."

She stared at her dame, completely aghast. "You cannot be serious, Mother!"

Had the countess' eyes shimmered before she looked away? "There is nothing objectionable about him, Victoria."

"Of course there is," she refuted hotly. "He's old, and stiff and..." she gulped, trying to find some other tangible quality that would make her mother dismiss him as a possible suitor. "And he, he looks at me in an unseemly way!"

Lady Ashford's gaze swung back, resting on her with such intensity, Tori nearly felt the need to confess her sins, both old and new. Remarkably she managed to hold her tongue and her poise.

"He is a man, Victoria, and you are both beautiful and charming. Looking at you is a natural instinct." A wan smile lifted her lips. "And he is not so old, really. Hardly much more than I."

This was too much. Tori leapt to her feet. "No, Mother, this is madness. Why? What is going on that you wish me to wed someone like him?" She narrowed her gaze. "No, not someone *like* him, you want me to marry the Colonel specifically. Why?"

A very visible tremor wracked the countess and her skin paled to an even whiter hue than usual before she regained control. "Family is most precious, Victoria. And you are already one and twenty. If you do not wed this season, then you may never do so. You will be a spinster. Alone, no children, no husband. Is that what you wish?"

Bitterness welled in her. No, a solitary life was most definitely not what she wanted. She wanted Matthew. But neither did she wish a staid, boring life with a man older than her late father. Before she could make another comment, her mother rose and hugged her close. "I only want you happy and safe, my dear. Please remember that, no matter what." She patted Tori's cheek. "Now, go upstairs and get some rest, you look wan."

"Mother, please." Tori gripped her mother's hands, squeezing. "Please tell me why."

"Go rest, Victoria." And, as so oft happened, her mother turned away.

"Who is Mr. Wolffe?" Tori called out.

Mother swayed the tiniest bit, one hand reaching out toward the wall before her back straightened even more and she turned the corner, moving out of sight.

Tori made for the sanctity of her room. Twisting the key, she secured the lock and leaned against the door, pondering both her mother's odd comments and the Colonel's visit. Something about the man caused warning bells to ring, but she could not quite decipher why.

He'd behaved the perfect gentleman. But his pointed looks and even more pointed comments did not sit well. She could not lie to herself, however. If Matthew made such subtly lascivious comments to her, she'd have the devil of a time not flinging herself at him, consequences be damned.

With a sigh, she pushed away from the door and rummaged in her wardrobe, digging beneath a mountain of hatboxes before pulling free her leather satchel.

True she had a ball to attend later this evening, but before that she owed her editor a new installment. What started as a lark had become a profitable, intoxicating adventure.

Three years earlier, she had discovered her brother's secret stash of *Opals* -- an underground paper of salacious adventures and sex—during a game of Blindman's Bluff. Time and again, she'd crept into his room while he was out and pilfered the papers, reading without truly understanding them. Laurel, of course, had been no help either. It had taken some time, covert eavesdropping and a good bit of bribery to the parlor maids for Tori to make sense of it all. Once she had, her newfound knowledge did more than thrill and titillate her, it roused her into a new awareness of everything and everyone around her. Including Matthew.

Most especially Matthew.

She began to notice how he moved, the way his eyes and hands spoke deeper than his words. Wondered and pictured how his body would entice and entangle with hers amid silken sheets and soft feather down. Soon, the stories of *The Opal* became almost ordinary. Though they still had the power to arouse, she found herself wanting more. Her imagination yielded hotter, more explicit visions of herself and Matthew.

At last, fantasy fueled by frustration drove her to pen her own salacious tale. Then another and another until one night, in a very tipsy whispered conversation with Laurel, she determined she would publish these stories. Despite the heady port, her friend had been aghast and rightfully so. The suggestion was ludicrous, even if Tori knew *how* one went about getting published.

Still, it was most tempting. Thrilling and forbidden. The heady temptation was too much for Tori's insouciant daring nature. First, she pinned down exactly when *The Opal* was delivered and how. That had been ridiculously easy. Finding the messenger boy and convincing him to carry an anonymous letter to the publisher had been more difficult –not to mention expensive. She'd had to coerce the little ragamuffin with nearly all her pin money.

Three years later, she – and the messenger – were both amassing a tidy sum from the writings. She paid him well for his silence, though he didn't know what her missives contained. Even her publisher had no idea of her identity.

In one dizzying swoop, she'd gone from innocent miss to published sex author. A career that, if discovered, would most definitely assure her ruination. No man, not even the Colonel – and definitely not Matthew—would wed her should the truth be known. And, despite her protestations to her mother, she did still pine for Matthew.

Tori pulled her thoughts away from both the Colonel and Matthew, settling herself down to write.

It was a pity, though, that her heroines received more salacious pleasure than she'd ever known. Likely ever would.

Innocent in real-world pleasures she may be, but her fictional characters and those of her fellow authors in *The Opal Chronicles* tutored her well. Gave her insight she'd wager no other unmarried miss of the Ton possessed. With that knowledge came a sort of instinct that told her Matthew Corwin would be a man to reckon with in the bedroom. If only... She sighed heavily, fearing such an arrangement would never occur between them. Matthew would marry a Diamond of the First Water. Someone elegant and blonde as a countess should be. Not a hoyden with salacious desires and a penchant for being daring and courting both disaster and ruin, even if she had a good family name and hefty dowry. Even with that knowledge, Matthew provided much needed inspiration and fantasy.

Pulling the leather folder open, she dug out her nib and parchment, re-reading the last bit she'd written.

Ewan's hand slid higher up her thigh, trembling over the silky flesh. He could smell her excitement, the honey already dripping from her cunny, wetting her thin linen chemise.

"My lord, it's frightfully hot in here. Why do you not disrobe?"

Ewan glowered at the upstairs maid. "I told you to stay silent. You'll have to pay for that."

The maid giggled before obviously remembering her role and assuming a pouting demeanor. "Pay, my lord?"

"Aye, wench." He slapped the inside of her thigh, cock tightening at her squeal. He traced the faint mark his palm left behind. "On your knees."

Her tits swayed deliciously as she complied, giving him a saucy wink over her shoulder, arse tilted at an enticing angle.

Ewan shifted behind her, running his fingertips along the backs of her legs up to her round, fleshy bottom. He pressed his palms flat against her. "Not quite warm enough, wench," he muttered, drew his hands back and brought one down, hard. Fast. Again and again until her delightful bum turned a rosy, splotchy hue of deepest red.

She screeched and flailed on the bed with each stroke of his hand, tears muffled by the pillows.

Tori shifted uncomfortably on the chair as she read, hand clenched at her lap, rubbing with slight pressure her own sensitive mound, visions of her characters replaced by herself and Matthew.

This was the sort of passion she wanted. The sort of lascivious, sexual heat that only a strong man could offer. A masterful man.

A man like Matthew Corwin.

Tori glanced at the gilded mantle clock and sucked in a sharp breath – she was literally running out of time. If she wished to receive her weekly payment, she must turn her manuscript over to the runner in less than an hour.

"Blast it," she muttered, bending once more over the parchment. Mind racing fast and naughty, she scribbled out a more than satisfying scene for Ewan and his maid, dabbling out the final words just as the clock rang the quarter hour.

"Hurry, hurry," she breathed, gathering up the papers, blowing over the last page to help the ink dry. She bundled the pages up in a neat, discreet package, donned her cloak and crept from the room.

Fortunately for her, the runner always showed up on time and in the same spot, an alleyway not more than two blocks from her house. Made getting in and out unnoticed much easier.

Delivery made, latest round of pound notes in hand, Tori started for home, sneaking in as quietly as she'd left. When she reached her room, she let out the breath she held, calmed her racing heart and stashed the money.

"Miss Victoria, are you awake?"

Glory's soft voice muffled its way through the thick oak door. Tori smoothed her hair and crossed to unlock the door to the upstairs maid.

"Yes, Glory, what is it?"

"Miss Edison would like a word."

Tori brightened, widening the door. "Send her up, please."

The maid left and moments later Laurel Edison took her place, face drawn and pinched with worry and fear?

"Laurel," Tori exclaimed moving forward. "Whatever is the matter? You're white as snow and twice as cold. Come by the fire." Laurel's body shook beneath her hands as Tori drew her further into the room.

"Shut the door," Laurel pleaded, fear thick in her voice. "Lock it, oh Tori, we're in deep trouble."

Her own sense of dread rising, Tori complied. "What's wrong?"

"Someone knows."

Tori gasped. "Impossible."

"No, it's true." Laurel dug in her pocket, producing a mangled bit of vellum. She held it out to Tori with a shaking hand.

"Oh God, oh God, oh God," Tori muttered at the threat slashed across the page. She raised stricken eyes to her friend. "When did this come? How did you get it?"

Tears spilled from Laurel's eyes. "A boy at market asked me if I was Miss Edison, friend of Miss Ashford. When I answered yes, he gave me this note and ran. Didn't even wait for a coin..." Laurel's voice trailed off, hiccupping slightly. She dragged in an audible, ragged gust of air. "Tori, what are we going to do? We'll be ruined."

Fear, dark and enveloping, more terrifying than anything she'd ever known, choked Tori.

Miss Ashford,

I know your secret. Unless you deliver to me 50 pounds, your mother will also discover the truth. Arrive at 9:00 tomorrow, southwest corner of Hyde Park, past the duck pond. Look for the tree wrapped with a green ribbon. I chose it to match your eyes.

~Fondest regards.

Bile rose in Tori's throat. She would be utterly ruined. More than ruined.

"Mayhap," she licked lips dry from fear. "Mayhap he does not speak of *The Opal*, at all." She flicked a nail along the edge of the blackmail note. "It could be anything he speaks of, Laurel, don't you think?"

Her friend stared at her as though she'd sprouted four arms and a third eye. "And what else have you done that would warrant a blackmail note, Victoria?" she ended on a near screech, pressing the back of her hand to her lips, drawing in a shuddering breath.

"Good point," Tori muttered, unable to argue the logic. Nor would she be able to argue with someone who'd ferreted her secret. For a brief moment she wondered if her messenger could have been responsible, but quickly abandoned that notion. He earned a handsome sum for his assistance. Though 50 pounds was a huge sum of money to someone in his position and the temptation would be strong. No. No, she refused to believe it was he.

Someone else knew.

Sick at both stomach and heart, she wadded the paper and stuffed it into her skirt pocket. "I suppose then, there's naught to be done but pay him."

Chapter Two

"WHOA, EASY, BOY," MATTHEW murmured when Orion tried to shift away from his questing fingers. A pebble caught beneath the horse's shoe, disrupting their early morning ride. The rising sun beat down through the trees, warming Matthew's neck and he loosened the buttons of his morning coat, tossing it atop the saddle.

Moments later, rock removed and coat slung over his arm, he walked through the dewy grass leading Orion. No sense putting any more weight on the horse's bruised flesh.

They came upon a deep curve in the pathway, both sides littered with dense trees. From the corner of his eye, he caught a flash of blue. Habit had him turning his head, to scan the area, but nothing moved. Still his senses vibrated with warning. Something, or someone, was out there, skulking through Hyde Park.

Guided by instinct honed in his years of service to the War Office, Matthew softly commanded the horse to stay. He shrugged back into his black morning jacket and slipped into the woods. The tracks of his quarry were easy enough to follow – scattered leaves in a straight line, crushed grass and displaced branches led him right ahead.

He looked up, catching the swish of dark blue fabric darting through the trees. With long, silent strides, he made up the distance between them then rounded out and up, passing his prey. Crouched behind the wide trunk of an ancient tree, Matthew caught the faint wheeze of breath, the hurried skip of shoes upon dried leaves. He waited until the last possible moment then leapt up, straight into the person's oncoming path.

However, he'd miscalculated slightly and they collided, falling to the ground in a tangled heap of curses.

Oh hell, a *soft* heap.

"Get off me, you oaf!"

Astonished, Matthew stared down into the snapping green eyes of Victoria Ashford.

"Matthew!" her pink mouth gaped briefly in surprise. "What are you doing? Are you following me?"

"Course not, I was out for a ride," he muttered distractedly. He still lay atop her, hands cupping her shoulders. Her cloak had come slightly askew, revealing the creaminess of her skin. He rubbed his thumb over the exposed flesh, feeling her tremble just a bit beneath him, catching her barely audible gasp. She was soft, touchable, delectable. Everything that somehow he knew she would be. With a start of surprise, he realized he wanted more. Wanted to trail his fingers from her shoulders to her breasts and fill his palms with her. His cock stiffened.

The rational part of him ordered him up and away from her instantly, but her full lush breasts pressed so temptingly to his chest prevented it. In their fall, she'd ended up in a rather inelegant sprawl and his hips nestled intimately between her legs.

How had he never noticed how long they were?

"Please, Matthew, get off."

God, but he wanted to. It would take no more than the simple pop of his button, a long, slow slide of her skirt and he could seat himself—"Damn it," he cursed, rolling off her and up in one lithe movement.

Reaching down, he yanked her to her feet. "What the hell are you doing out here this time of day?" Matthew sought any direction but hers and scanned the area. "Where is your maid?"

Tori swatted at bits of leaves and brambles clinging to her and waved toward the north end of the park. "She's just beyond there," she bit out, though her voice wobbled. "Where's your horse?"

He snapped his head back to her, control firmly in place. "Answer the question."

She edged away, hand patting her skirt, green eyes darting behind him. "I did, she's over there. Now, if you'll excuse me, I should be off."

Suspicion clouded him and he grabbed hold of her arm, preventing flight. "What are you doing here, Victoria? Meeting a lover, perhaps?"

The thought burned him. "A morning assignation?"

Her cheeks flushed and her eyes widened seconds before she swung at him, landing a decent blow to his cheek. "How dare you!"

Matthew glowered and yanked her to him. She clutched at his shoulders for support, again flattening her breasts into him.

"Answer me, damn you."

"No, of course not," she yelled, trying to pull away.

The friction only roused him more. In that moment he didn't give a damn who could round the corner of their secluded spot and find them, his only thought to savor and taste her mouth. Sliding his arm around her waist, he splayed his fingers over the swell of her buttocks.

Tori arched, fingers spasming around his shoulders. She licked her lips. "Oh my. Matthew?"

"Then what?" he whispered, bending his head.

He had to taste her. Just once. She would be sweet. Innocent.

"I... I just, I don't know. What are you doing?"

"I'm going to kiss you."

"Finally," she muttered, threading her fingers into his hair, face lifting to meet him halfway.

Matthew brushed a gentle kiss over her mouth, savoring her gasp, her tremors. Sweet, pure.

Widening his stance, he slipped his other hand beneath her tumbled down hair, stroking the back of her neck, his thumb urging her chin up.

He deepened the pressure, her mouth soft and full like her breasts. Wet and filled with the sweet taste of her morning chocolate. He was so damn hard he could take her standing up.

She moaned and tugged at his hair. "Matthew," she murmured, "More, please."

The sound of his name on her lips brought him back to reality with an unpleasant thump. Jerking away, he took three steps back. What was he thinking? This was Victoria. An innocent.

"You never explained why you were out here."

She blinked, several times, head tipped to the side studying him as if he were a prized insect on a pin. A pink flush stained her cheeks once more, but she did not drop her gaze.

"You kissed me."

Forcing himself to show absolutely no emotion, he cocked a brow. "I've kissed a lot of women."

What could have been a flinch crossed her face, but with a set jaw and stubbornness in her eyes, she stepped forward and poked him in the chest. "I am not a lot of women. *Why* did you kiss me?"

Hell, if he knew that he wouldn't have done it. "Opportunity and it's high past time you were kissed."

Her nostrils flared. "Opportunity, is it?" she growled. "And who is to say that was my first kiss?"

"Trust me," he snarled back, "I can tell."

Her luscious mouth fell open and her face flushed deeply. A pang hit him and he shrugged irritably. He had to get her off this subject. The tint of her ire brought a sparkle to her eyes that was damn near enchanting, but more detrimental to his control was the way her agitated breaths caused her chest to rise and fall. "Now, for the last time, what are you doing out here? I suggest you answer," he snapped, more than eager to be away. "I'm damn near out of patience with you."

"Oh, you bloody, ridiculous, obtuse man!" Her fists balled and he thought she might try to hit him again, but instead, she jerked her chin toward the path. "I'm out for a walk, now if you'll excuse me, I must be going."

And she moved past him. Long confident strides that both annoyed and amused him. He caught up with her in seconds, but refrained from touching her again.

Odd things happened when he did that. Things he didn't expect, didn't want, and refused to examine. Tori was meant for marriage to a man who would love her blindly. "Might I ask where we are going?"

She did not look at him, merely continued her march. "*We* are not going anywhere. *I* am going here. *You* may leave."

Matthew chuckled. No one, even before he inherited his brother's title, had dismissed him. And quite so snidely, too.

"Victoria," he began, but she cut him off.

"You're right, it meant nothing, Matthew, do not give it another thought. I certainly won't."

God would surely strike her down for such a whopping lie, but Tori could not stand to see the pity she knew would be in his eyes. He could tell she'd never been kissed. How mortifying. Had she truly done it so badly?

"Go away," she hissed, desperate for him to be gone. Not only was he an appalling distraction, but she had to find the correct location. Why had it always sounded so breathlessly exciting in her novels? Dealing with a blackmailer was anything but.

Where was it? Blast Matthew and his untimely interference. The tumble and subsequent kissing had robbed her of her directional abilities. Faint voices from the filling park trickled through the trees behind her. She started forward in the opposite directions, throat constricted. Would the blackmailer still be there?

"You look mighty determined," Matthew noted from beside her.

She stopped, quelling him with a glare. At least she tried to. Unfortunately, it had no effect on him. She was torn between re-living every second, every sensation of his kiss – good Lord it was still unbelievable that he'd done such a thing! – and dealing with the more immediate threat.

"Do you think," she began quite softly, "that you could be so good as to leave me be? I've a very important errand and you are not allowed."

Allowed? Lud, but she sounded like a schoolroom twit.

"Sorry, Tori," though he sounded anything but. "I cannot in good conscience allow you to wander the darkened woods of Hyde Park without some sort of protection."

Guiltily she clutched her reticule tighter. God only knew what would happen should he discover she carried her pistol. Just in case.

Tori swallowed hard. "Who is to protect me from you? You know what would happen should we be discovered alone." He blanched and she smirked at her tiny bit of revenge, ignoring the pain of truth. Even though he'd kissed her, Matthew obviously did not wish anything more. Most definitely not marriage. "I'm perfectly safe. Please, *go*."

"Call your maid, then. Better yet, return home. Surely this *errand* is not worth your reputation."

Heavens, if he only knew.

Biting her lip, she closed her eyes. "Do you have the time?"

"Quarter past nine, if you can believe it. I thought you didn't rise until ten at the earliest?"

After nine! Oh no, she was very late. This could not be good.

She sprinted ahead, searching each copse of trees for the tell tale green ribbon tied around the base of a trunk. Her heart sank when she spied it at last. Glancing about, she didn't see anyone loitering nearby. Had he gone, then? Given up on the exchange? She didn't think so as the oddest sensation swept over her. For once, the prickle at the back of her neck had nothing to do with Matthew.

He was here. Watching.

The flutter of a small square envelope caught her eye. Swooping down, she picked it up, shoving it into her pocket near the packet of money and worked at freeing the ribbon.

"What did you find?"

She gritted her teeth, turned around and dangled the fabric at him.

"That's it?" he asked in disbelief. "All that fuss and bother for a bit of fluff?"

"Yes," she insisted, hand hovering over her pocket.

"Try again. What is on the note you picked up?"

She gasped and backed away a couple of steps. "N-n-nothing."

With a quick, blurred movement, Matthew reached into her dress pocket. She batted at his hand and they grappled briefly then froze at the sound of fabric tearing. Looking down, Tori saw the rip at her shoulder, her bare skin peeking through. She gasped and glanced at Matthew, catching the flick of awareness in his eyes.

"Miss Ashford, where are you?" Glory hissed from behind them, leaves rustling beneath her oncoming steps. "Someone is coming!"

One hand clutching at her shoulder, Tori spun around even as Matthew sprang backward. Oh no!

Biting her lip, she looked at Matthew, but he was gone. Disappeared.

"What the deuce?"

"Miss Ashford," Glory hissed again, the fear in her voice loud.

"Here, Glory." She hurried forward, turning the maid away from where they'd stood. She had no idea where Matthew was, but she didn't want to chance his being seen.

"What happened to your dress?" the maid asked.

"I fell," Tori responded, flicking her gaze left and right as they walked. The unease still surrounded her. It was only when they reached the safety of the now-populated path that she realized with horror she'd failed to leave the money.

Tori turned her head, swallowing hard. She could not go back now. Perhaps he would give her another chance. She tapped her pocket, breathing a sigh of relief at the crackle of paper. At least she still had the note.

Arriving safely home, they slid past Ryder's study and into her bedroom.

"Glory, this is our secret, right?"

The girl looked at her with wary eyes. "Are you truly all right? Nothing happened?"

"No, I swear."

With obvious reluctance, the maid slowly nodded. "Right then, we need to get you out of this dress."

The change was quickly made and Glory gathered up the torn dress. "I'll fix the seam."

"No, no." Tori tugged it away. The note was still in the pocket. "I'll do it, Glory. It was my fault. Really, I insist."

A confused smile touched the maid's lips but she relinquished the gown. "All right, Miss."

Once she'd left, Tori shut and locked the door. So much had happened in one hour, the most astonishing of all was Matthew. She pressed her fingers to her mouth in wonderment.

Matthew Corwin kissed her. He'd touched and held her and his eyes gleamed with passion, with desire. Despite his churlish comment, she knew he'd felt something, too. He must have.

"Incredible, truly amazing." With a light laugh, she drifted across her room, sinking into the small chair at her escritoire. Would he do it again? She wanted him to.

Even better, Matthew's kiss had proven to her no matter what her mother said no other man would do for her husband.

Since she could not write for *The Opal* any longer, she would employ all her creative devices into enticing Matthew into marriage. One kiss would lead to another and another then definitely into the depths of passion she both read and wrote about.

It was a brilliant plan. Tori decided she would begin this very night at the Harrington ball.

The hall clock chimed the ten o'clock hour, snapping her from her reverie. Laurel would be arriving any moment for her report.

One she didn't have to give. Not of the blackmailer certainly and she could not tell her about Matthew, his kiss a precious secret she very much wanted to keep to herself.

Secrets.

She remembered the note left behind. Tugging it free, she stared at her initials scrawled along the top edge. The dark, black ink chilled her. Setting the envelope on her desk, she stood up and paced back and forth, sending occasional suspicious glances at the note.

She really did not want to open it. How unlike her. Still, no matter how she chastised herself, the note remained untouched. She would wait for Laurel and they would read it together.

Needing a distraction, she returned to the desk, edged the note beneath a pile of correspondence and pulled out a fresh piece of paper. She would craft a Plan of Seduction. One to win his hand in marriage. It was perfect. She would cater to his every need and taste. Writing the words with bold, underlined strokes, she added his name with a flourish. Tori nibbled on the end of her quill, thinking back on the many stories from the *Opal.* What would he like?

Matthew was a highly sexual man. Though it seemed she'd always known this instinctively, years of watching him had fortified that knowledge. More than once she'd caught him with a widow in the gardens of some party, though he never saw her. Heavens that would have been awkward. She never had been very good at concealing her emotions and she was positive he would have noticed both her fury and jealousy – two things she knew he despised.

But even the knowledge he was with another woman couldn't quell her curiosity or her need for him.

Once, she'd even followed him to a brothel. Not that one would ever know the upscale apartment house in the middle of Grosvenor Square was anything but the house of a well-off widow. It was only by chance – oh very well, by her adeptness at eavesdropping – that she even discovered its existence. During a low-voiced conversation with her brother, she heard Matthew making his plans and made some of her own.

It had been terrifying and exhilarating. Dressed as a lad, face scrubbed with coal dust and hair shoved 'neath a tweed cap, she'd darted behind him staying to the shadows until he walked up the stairs and disappeared inside.

Frustrated by her lack of visibility, Tori skirted the building, approaching the rear doors. Unfortunately, they'd been locked. Until a garbage boy opened one and stepped out and down the alley, leaving the door slightly ajar.

Even now she remembered how her heart pounded so loudly she was certain she'd be caught, the sweat pooling between her bound breasts. Nerves shook her entire body, but she was dying to see the inside of the house.

Just a peek. Before she had time to change her mind, she slipped inside, ducking quickly through the busy kitchen.

No one paid her any mind. Through a long hallway Tori followed muffled sounds until footsteps alerted her to someone's approach. She yanked open a narrow door, peered into the nearly black interior, then ducked inside when she ascertained it empty.

The footsteps passed, but just as she was about to leave the sounds of moaning caught her attention. The small room held only a stool and a square of velvet draped over two walls. Ever curious, Tori lifted one of the panels revealing a hole no bigger than a strawberry. The tempo of the moans increased and she leaned forward, pressing her eye to the hole.

A bed was situated right in her line of sight. On it was a man and woman, both naked. The woman straddled the man whose thin, pale hands wrapped around lithe hips, guiding her up and down.

Her back arched and her breasts swayed side to side. Tori pressed even closer, hoping for a glimpse of what the woman was riding, but their movements were so fast it was impossible.

Suddenly the man slammed hard and groaned, holding the woman tightly to his groin. Tori saw a heaving shudder wrack the woman and her head dropped to his shoulder. She shook her lower body, eliciting an appreciative murmur from the man beneath her.

"Another one, luv?"

His hands delved into the furrow of her bottom, but his response was too low for Tori to hear.

She pulled away and dropped the curtain, her entire body humming. So that's what it was really all about.

She couldn't wait to get home to write about it, after caring for her own arousal, of course. Watching the actual act of penetration had done something to her that demanded release.

Getting out of the brothel had its own trials including an encounter with a tipsy whore who tried to kiss her, but she'd squirmed free and was shimmying up to her room in no time.

Laurel had been scandalized. And perhaps a wee bit jealous.

Tori grinned again at the memory. That had been one of her best-selling serials in *The Opal* – voyeurism was very popular. To this day she could well understand why.

"I wonder if Matthew likes to watch?" The notion did not set well with her – watching meant more than one woman and she was not about to allow that.

Scratching out several other ideas on her Plan of Seduction filled the time until Laurel showed up, breathless and late.

"Sorry," she murmured, dropping her bonnet on the bed. "I couldn't get away. How did it go?"

Tori carefully arranged her Plan out of sight and pulled free the note card.

"Not well, I'm afraid."

She related the Matthew incident, omitting the kiss and showed her the envelope.

"What does it say?" Laurel asked, voice laced with enough dread to make any actress proud.

"I don't know, I haven't opened it."

They stared at each other over the parchment, identical expressions of worry on their faces. "Well, go on, then, do it," Laurel prompted.

Tori nodded, slit it open and pulled out the card. It was short and quite pointed.

Miss Ashford,

A whore's secret does not remain secret for long. The price of my silence is now 100 pounds. Return tomorrow at 9:00 sharp. Come alone, your maid may again wait at the edge of the path.

~Fondest regards.

Re-reading, the words took on new meaning for Tori.

"Laurel, Laurel!" She nudged her friend, pinching her arm til she roused from her near-faint. Laurel always had been a bit dramatic. "You must quit this idiocy. I have figured out the meaning of the notes."

Her friend frowned, rubbing at her arm. "It's not hard, Tori, he wants money or he'll ruin you."

"No, no, that is not it. Well, that *is* it, but I don't think he's talking about *The Opal.*" She paced again, something that never seemed to work to help her think, but always to speak logically. "He specifically mentions the word *whore.* Don't you see, he knows nothing about my writings, but must know about my trip to Lizzeth's!"

Laurel's mouth gaped before snapping shut with an audible click. "That is not any better, Victoria! You'll still be ruined if it gets out."

Still true. Drat.

"Yes, but at least now I can pay him off but I won't have to quit *The Opal.*"

"Good God, don't tell me you are going write, yet? Have you not had enough of a scare for one lifetime?" Laurel jumped up, pacing right alongside her. "This is madness. *You* are mad, completely devoid of all sensibilities. Pay him. Quit writing. Do not visit any more of those places. Marry a nice, boring earl or viscount and live the rest of your days in security."

It was quite a speech coming from her often timid friend. Tori had become accustomed to being the leader of the two, but times like these reminded her of the spark Laurel held. She grimaced.

"Truly? Stop writing?"

"Yes," Laurel dragged the word out, ending on such a note of obvious disgust that Tori could not help but laugh.

"All right, all right, you win. Tomorrow morning, I shall return to the park and leave the money, then we will be done with this."

"Promise?"

Tori bit her lip, looked away for a moment then shrugged. "Trust me, I do not wish to live in a convent nor be shipped to the Americas."

Laurel appeared both satisfied and immensely relieved. "Thank you." She threw her arms around Tori and hugged her tight.

For her part, Tori did not look too closely at the fact that she had not *actually* promised her friend anything other than the fact she would despise the consequences of discovery.

Truly, it was a small difference. Besides, it would appear she had no need of *The Opal* any longer – she had a Plan.

Chapter Three

"ALL RIGHT MY LORD, now that you have me out here, what is your plan?"

Matthew chuckled, running his finger over the exposed skin of his companion's neck. Goosebumps rose and she could not conceal her excitement. "What do you want me to do, Mrs. Banford?"

The pretty blonde widow shuddered delicately and edged closer, pushing her cleavage upward, her tits nearly falling out of her dress.

"Whatever you wish to do to me, my lord." Mrs. Banford's lashes swept down in provocative feigned shyness. "I am yours to command."

Unexpectedly he heard the words uttered in Tori's voice; it was her perfect handfuls of breasts against his chest, her startling green eyes acquiescing to him. The imagery made his cock jerk. Matthew refocused on the petite *available* widow before him. "Are you now?" he asked huskily.

"Mm-hmm."

He lowered his head, fingers tangling in her hair, nudging her head backward. She was ripe for the taking, but was she truly willing to play the game? He tugged harder.

"Ow! Curse it, Sussex, have a care! My maid spent hours on this style." She jerked away with a huff.

A light quickly smothered laugh floated to him. Matthew cut a dark look at the doors leading from the balcony where they stood to the well-lit ballroom. He didn't see her, but he knew Tori was about somewhere. Little minx. Would she always plague him now?

"I believe it is time for us to return, Mrs. Banford."

The widow gaped at him, still fiddling with her damn hair. He squelched a burst of irritation and held his arm to her.

"But I thought we were going to..." she waved her hands. "Aren't we?"

"No." Offering no further explanation, he took her elbow and propelled her inside, his keen gaze still sweeping the balcony, piercing the darkened shadows, but he did not see Tori.

Matthew deposited Mrs. Banford at the refreshment table and left, intent on finding Tori. She stood just behind her mother's chair, a flush staining her cheeks, chest rising just a bit faster than was usual. Nerves or the result of her hasty return?

"Lord Sussex." Lady Ashford inclined her head. "How good to see you. Surprising, one might say."

"I could not disappoint Miss Ashford, my lady. I believe this dance is mine?"

The countess started. "I was unaware, my lord. It is a waltz, you know."

He saw Tori look down at the dangling card her mouth moving as she silently read the names. "Oh but—,"

"With your permission?" But he didn't wait, merely took Tori's arm and led her away to the ballroom floor. He slid one arm about her waist, clasping her gloved fingers with light firmness. "What were you doing on the balcony?" He kept his voice low. A scandal involving Tori was the last thing he needed.

Her eyes met his and she raised her chin slightly. "What were *you* doing out there?" she challenged in return.

"Do you really wish to know?"

Her spine stiffened beneath his fingers, green fire snapped in her eyes. "I am no fool, Matthew, I know exactly what you were about with that woman."

He paused as they waltzed past another couple. Expertly, he guided her through the crowded dance floor to the furthest edge.

"Is that why you were there?" he finally murmured, drawing her a bit closer, inhaling her light scent. Flowery and subtle. She felt warm and vibrant. "Did you want to watch?"

The sharp talons of her fingertips dug into his shoulder even as her gaze shuttered. "Watch what, my lord? You make yet another conquest? No, thank you."

Matthew studied her downcast lashes. Neither shy nor demure, there was another reason she hid her eyes. A different sort of awareness seemed to thrum below her surface, just under his palm.

Impossible. It was his own unsatisfied desires which made him think she had any sensual awareness. His own visions of Tori naked and obedient which threatened his carefully honed control.

For his own sanity, he must put an end to whatever ideas their kiss had stirred within her. And himself. She was strictly off-limits.

A good set-down to repel her and he would have no more worries on that front. But before he could speak, she asked him the most incredulous question.

"Do *you* like to watch?"

Her eyes met his again, still burning and intense.

"What the devil?" Matthew spun her too quickly for the tempo of the music, placing his back to the crowd who watched them. "What the ... what kind of question is that?"

"You asked me," she retorted pertly, tossing her head.

"That's different," he ground out. "I know what I'm talking about. You'd better not have a damn idea."

"Why? Because I'd never been kissed before you? That may be true and I may need practice at it, but I do have some understanding of what goes on between men and women. I am twenty-one, you know. And we have quite, uh active maids who don't always keep their conversations to themselves."

"Oh for God's sake," he bit out, steering her outside to the balcony. Thankfully it was empty, though he knew it would not remain so for long. Catching her by the shoulders, he gave her a light shake. "You don't need any sort of practice, kissing or otherwise."

Lifting her hands to his chest, she smoothed the lapels of his jacket, licking her bottom lip when she looked up at him. No shade of doubt shone in her mesmerizing green eyes.

"Are you saying you like the way I kiss?"

Her voice dropped, wrapping around him like a sultry hand. It did things to his body she really should not be able to do. This was Victoria.

Son of a bitch.

"Listen, whatever ideas you have about me forget them. There is nothing for you here."

She stepped closer, nestling against him, an innocent siren bent on his undoing. Damned if it wasn't working, too. His cock rose, buoyed by his excellent view of her breasts. Matthew really wanted to taste her again, to suckle away the sheen left by her tongue.

"Matthew, it doesn't feel like there's nothing there."

To his great astonishment, she gently pressed her hips forward. Her eyes widened and a pink blush darkened her cheeks, but she didn't move back.

He gritted his teeth, shocked to his toes, seeking words.

"In fact, I'd say there's quite *a lot* there," Tori whispered.

Matthew pushed her away. "The overheard whispers of maids don't mean a thing, Victoria. Your behavior is unacceptable."

He saw the hurt and mortification strip away her flirtatious demeanor and damned near apologized. He didn't like causing her pain, but knew it was for the best. He had to end this now. "Since you know so much, Miss Ashford, undoubtedly you will understand when I tell you that I require a woman of more... sophisticated tastes and abilities."

The moonlight broke from a cloud, bathing her white face, making it appear even more stark. "I see." She drew herself up, affecting an air of dispassion.

"I'm glad that you do," he said.

"Oh yes," she graced him with a frosty smile. "I see that you are arrogant beyond all comprehension, Corwin. Or perhaps my mild flirtation meant a bit too much to you. I did but practice upon you."

He inclined his head, allowing her words. What harm was there in saving her pride? "Practice."

"Oh yes. I mean, you are older – quite a bit older than me – and very much a rake. Who better than to learn a few tricks from? I've my eye on a few different gentlemen this Season who would make excellent husbands. And though he does surpass you in age, my mother assures me the Colonel is quite interested in making a match with me. Perhaps I shall indulge him." She turned and strode to the ballroom doors. Fingers on the handle, she looked back at him. "Thank you for the lessons, I'm positive they'll be put to good use."

Tori's parting shot burned his temper completely away. He'd had enough, had done his damn duty tonight. Striding around the wide veranda, he found another entrance, intent on leaving with all possible haste.

Instead, he was waylaid by first one marriage-minded mama, then another. In between, he caught glimpses of Tori laughing and flirting her way through a bevy of attentive young bucks. His anger burned and simmered. Twenty minutes later, he finally escaped into a side corridor he knew led to Lord Harrington's study. Opening the door, he caught the faint murmur of voices and a startled feminine gasp, but the light was too low for him to make anyone out.

"My apologies," he growled in their vicinity, starting to pull the door closed. Damn, but he could have used a brace of brandy and respite from the bloodhounds dancing in the ballroom.

"Corwin, come in!"

It was Ashford's voice. Relieved, Matthew pushed back inside, closing the door with an emphatic click. An echoing *snick* came from the opposite side of the room. An oil lamp burned low on a side table, the room brightening as Ashford turned up the wick. He was alone.

Matthew gave his friend a wry grin. "Sorry for interrupting. Nothing you can't resume later, I assume?"

"There will be other opportunities." Ryder shrugged, scrutinizing him intently. "What are you about?"

"Biding my time before I take my leave. Several determined mothers have the exits blocked so well a man can hardly move without them taking note."

Ryder chuckled. "Will you go to the club when you leave here?"

Since the incident with Tori on the balcony he'd been on edge. He needed to relieve the sexual energy burning in him. "No," he stated firmly. "I'm going to Lizzeth's. She sent round a note the other day about a new girl she thought would suit me."

Ashford's gaze flicked to the door next to him for an instant. "I see."

"Care to join me?" They'd often journeyed to the whorehouse together, though they'd never shared women. Matthew did not share.

"No, I think not. I've an early morning meeting with Lord Richter about a horse he's keen on selling."

Matthew checked his pocket watch. A quarter past midnight. The revelers populating the Harrington ball, including Tori and her adoring peacocks, would be well-occupied for another few hours. By the time they fell into their beds, he'd have taken his unique brand of pleasure several times over.

And still thirst for more. Damn the minx and her newfound abilities to arouse him.

Tori pulled her burning ear away from the door separating her from the two men in the study.

He was going back to the whorehouse.

Strong, powerful hurt clouded her mind. She didn't want him to bed anyone else. It wasn't in the Plan.

Slipping out of the adjoining room, she scurried back into the ballroom ideas whirling feverishly. How could her Plan of Seduction work if he wasn't around to be seduced?

A waiter passed by with a tray of champagne. Taking two, she downed them in quick succession. Ironically, the drinks seemed to strengthen both her resolve and her options. Of course, it was simple. Brilliant, even.

She found her mother and made her excuses, pleading a headache. Though she was loath to leave, the countess finally acquiesced and within minutes they were rattling home in their carriage.

"Did Ryder speak with you about the Colonel?"

Their dance had been stilted and tedious. Tori rolled her eyes. "Yes."

"And you will accept his suit?"

"Of course not," she spouted, straightening in her seat, clutching the edge rail with a strong grip. "He's old and repulsive. I'll not marry him, no matter what Father promised you."

Her mother's sharp in-drawn breath held annoyance. "You'll do as you are bade, Victoria. This is not a matter of inconsequence."

The carriage bumped and bounced over the cobblestones. "Is it so difficult to understand that I wish to marry for love?" Tori finally said. "Like you and Father?"

"Such matches are rare, dear heart." Her mother leaned forward, clutching at Tori's hands, a look of almost-panic on her face. "Please, love, if nothing else, then humor him for a bit. Perhaps another, better offer shall come this Season, but until then...?"

The uncertainty on her mother's face tore at her heart. But secure in her new Plan for winning Matthew's heart and hand in marriage, she cautiously nodded. She could afford a few days to pacify the Colonel. "All right."

A sigh of relief bounced in the carriage. "Excellent. You'll not regret this, Victoria."

"I shall be right as rain in the morning, Mother, I promise," Tori said when they finally reached the house. Handing her wrap to the maid, she practically bolted up the stairs.

"All right, but do not forget the Colonel is calling on you at eleven."

Tori skidded to a halt on the landing, peering over the railing at her mother. "You didn't? I only just said I'd consider his suit!"

"He is well-connected and wealthy. The Colonel is a good match."

The champagne buzzed in her ears, whispering insidious notions to her. Tori batted them away. "I'll go, Mother," she said. "But nothing more. You must not set your mind that I will marry him."

The countess rubbed at her temples, her eyes shadowed and hidden. "What's done cannot be undone. Get some rest, Victoria. We'll discuss this more tomorrow."

Tori nibbled at her lip before nodding and practically sprinting up the stairs. She had only a few moments to put the next phase of her Plan into action. It may cost her dearly, but she saw no other way.

She would take the money intended for the morrow's payoff and switch places with the new whore at Lizzeth's. A mask, a disguised voice and Matthew would not know it was she awaiting him in bed.

It was a daring, nay ridiculous scheme, but Tori's intuition told her this might very well be her best -- her only—chance at securing Matthew's affections. Especially with her mother bent on this hideous match with the Colonel.

The idea of his touch, his hands, his kiss repelled her more than she could express. God forbid she would have to suffer that. And if she did by some unfortunate stroke of fate, at least she would have this night to always remember true passion.

As Glory unlaced her dress, she went through the Plan once again, seeking problems finding many gaping holes. Ones she would deal with as they arose. The important thing was getting to the whorehouse before Matthew did.

Everything would sort itself out, she was confident. With a little help, and some planning, it always did.

"GOOD EVENING, MY LORD. It is a pleasure to see you again. It has been much too long."

Matthew turned as Lizzeth, the petite madam, swept inside. He bowed over her hand. "I apologize, but I admit your letter has piqued my interest."

She chuckled warmly. "I thought it might. When she arrived, my first thought was of you."

Matthew's body immediately took interest, his cock hardening. "How experienced is she?" While some of the other girls took his tastes in stride, they didn't always get the same satisfaction he did and though that wasn't a necessity, it made the act more enjoyable. More rewarding.

"She's had a few, but not so many she'll lie there flat whilst you finish. She's a quiet little miss, almost timid, but she's a right true girl."

"Good, send for her."

Lizzeth hesitated. "Listen my lord, you know how my girls are, always fighting over you. I'm in no mood for that, tonight. I'll line them up in the Captain's room and you pick. She'll be the last to your right."

Matthew chuckled, nodding. "All right, Lizzeth, go get them ready."

"Good. I'll come for you shortly."

He spent the next fifteen minutes anticipating what the night held, mingled with flashes of unwanted memories – all featuring a small, dark-haired urchin he watched grow into a beautiful woman.

The door opened and Lizzeth beckoned him forward. She caught his arm as he passed, a puzzled frown on her face. "She's taken to wearing a mask tonight, my lord, said she'd feel more *obedient*."

The mere word raised his cock once more and he grinned with wolfish glee. "Perfect." Settling a well-filled purse in her hand, Matthew stepped through the door, picked up the riding crop Lizzeth left and approached the four girls who awaited him.

They presented an erotic display for his hungry eyes. Dressed only in thin chemises, the women were bent over a low table, arses up, heads down and legs slightly spread. Right away he recognized two of them, both of whom he'd enjoyed in the past. Letting his excitement rise and peak, Matthew refrained from looking at the last girl, gaze roaming over the third – a blonde he didn't remember having. She looked over her shoulder at him and winked, her rouged mouth thin and wide. And vastly talented at coaxing an orgasm. Oh yes, now he recognized that face and mouth. A good time, but not the one tonight.

However, he had a role to play. Forcing a scowl to his face, he moved closer and smacked her smartly on the ass. "Eyes forward, wench."

The girls giggled and wiggled, each trying to entice him to choose her. All save the fourth one. She remained mostly still, though her hips swayed lightly and her shoulders shook with a fine, nearly invisible tremor. Her head was low to the table and she had what appeared to be a white-knuckled grip on it.

He smelled her submissiveness and it shot straight to his cock.

Unable to resist her allure any further, Matthew eyed her with lustful curiosity. Long, curly black hair, shoved haphazardly into some sort of queue and wound with a green ribbon, spilled down her slender back. Matthew drew a deep breath, blinked away the image of Tori and stroked himself, easing some of the pressure building in his breeches. Long, lean legs peeked out from the ruffled edges of her white, almost pristine chemise and her derriere appeared firm and lush.

He wondered if it had ever been taken.

Moving along the line of girls, he slapped the crop against his palm, the small sound of leather on flesh causing more jumps, giggles and groans. He enjoyed this part of it almost as much as he enjoyed taking them. Anticipation of the unknown, wondering how far he'd go, how much the taste of the crop on bare flesh would sting.

Randomly, he reached out and fondled them, slid his hand over a well rounded bottom, pinched a fleshy thigh, nipped at an available shoulder until at last, he could take no more and stood directly behind his choice for the night. Wedging a foot between her legs, he leaned down and whispered in her ear, "Wider."

She jerked and moaned, a near-violent tremble rushing through her. "Sir?" she asked, confusion in her voice.

With one hand braced in the small of her back forcing her further into the table, he pushed at her foot. "Open your legs wider."

The room became breathless, the scuff of her bare feet almost inaudible as she moved.

One of the other girls groaned. "Oh, no fair, 'e's takin' the new'un."

The other two chimed in with a chorus of disappointment, which Matthew quickly quelled, tossing each girl a coin. "Go on now, rest up or find another gent to entertain and take your mind off of me. There'll be other times."

The women giggled, pressed friendly hands to his back and bum, whispered good luck to the young vixen still trembling beneath his hand and left the room.

When the door shut, Matthew withdrew slowly, watching his companion as she lay against the table. The tremors that pulsed through her gave him pause until he noticed the dampness between her legs. The thin white linen of her chemise turned nearly transparent, wetted by the juices of her arousal.

He smiled.

"Don't move," he said, striding to the door and locking it. Pausing only long enough to draw a deep breath and some control, Matthew returned to her, admiring her shapely buttocks and legs once more.

Truly the lines of a well-bred filly. One he intended to ride hard.

He stepped between her legs again, nestling the length of his clothed, distended cock in the cleft of her arse. Leaning down, he used the weight of his body to press her further into the table, flattening her, knowing the pressure on her breasts must border on erotic pain. Just enough to stimulate her and it appeared to work. She moaned and wiggled slightly, head shifting to the right, nearly looking back at him. Gathering a fistful of silky black hair careful not to dislodge the ribbon holding her mask, he pulled, lowering his mouth to her ear. A hint of lavender filled his senses, a tantalizing hint of innocence and seduction.

"Lizzeth tells me you're accustomed to this sort of play. That you enjoy it. Is that true?"

"I," she swallowed so hard he heard it. "Yes."

He inhaled sharply, his cock twitching with her response. "How much can you take?"

Another tremor, another deep breath. "I don't know," she said so softly, he had to strain to catch her words. "No man has ever really pushed me."

Matthew contemplated her statement with a sense of erotic elation. She issued a challenge he could not refuse.

Pulling her back further with his grip on her hair, Matthew tapped her flank with the crop. "You will take the whip?"

"Aye," the word came quickly, accompanied by a roll of her hips.

"You will obey me, no matter what I ask of you." Not a question this time.

"Yes, sir."

Matthew very nearly growled with pleasure.

"I do have one request, sir."

"Speak."

"You may use me in any fashion, and I will obey your every command, but please, do not remove my mask."

He gave a sharp tug at her hair, eliciting a pained groan. "Who is the master here?"

"You are, but please, grant me, on your honor as a gentleman, this one request."

Matthew removed himself from her, eyeing the beauty spread so submissively before him. Her body was his to do with as he pleased and knowing she was so sexually charged by his dominance made it all the sweeter. Never had he had a partner equal his passion for this particular amusement. Giving her this safety would not detract from the night's pleasure and mayhap would only enhance it.

"Very well, but you will pay a price for daring to ask such a thing." He tapped the crop against the inside of her thigh, pleased when she automatically spread her legs further, muscles strained and taut. "I will not permanently harm you, but you will leave my bed this night marked."

Her soft moan made him want to plunge into her full force. "Yes, sir, I understand."

"Your penance for asking will be five strikes with the crop. My agreement will cost you ten more." He bent the flexible leather whip in his hands, debating where to let it fall first. "No need to count them this time."

Running a tender, caressing hand over her sleek cheeks he slid his fingers beneath the linen chemise and yanked it upward so it pulled taut against her clitoris and the tight furrow of her arse. She barely had time to gasp before he brought the crop down on the now totally bare flesh, leaving a bright red stripe.

She yelped, hands reaching back to cover herself.

Quickly, Matthew pinned them down. "I can see I shall have to restrain you."

"Oh, no, sir, please."

"Five more," he rasped, wondering how he would last through the punishment before taking her. He was so hard he hurt.

Yanking his cravat from his neck, Matthew wound the material around her hands, preventing her from interfering further. "We begin again." He brought the crop down quickly, enflamed by the sound of leather on her tender flesh and the arousing sight of her striped skin.

Tori cringed and moaned with each strike, though the core of her body threatened to overheat and explode. Never before had she felt such pressure, such need, between her legs. The urge to orgasm was so strong, she could barely control it. She could hardly believe she was here, in a whorehouse, allowing Matthew to treat her with less than anything resembling decency.

Or that she was so aroused by it, that she could spend over and over again.

All the bawdy words and terms she'd written rushed into her head. She wanted to spout them to him, to beg him to make her come, but knew to do so would incite refusal and more punishment.

Every midnight fantasy she'd entertained, every naughty, lascivious thought she'd had was coming true. Only so much more terrifying and exciting than she'd ever imagined.

The crop lashed down on her tender arse again and she groaned, grinding her hips to the table in an attempt at some sort of respite. The sting was addictive.

"Ah, ah, ah," he murmured, his low, familiar baritone close to her ear. "None of that, my pretty little whore. You'll not spend unless I allow it, understand?"

Whore. This time the word tantalized her, sending an even greater ache to throb between her legs.

Matthew's strong body pressed firmly against hers, his hand sweeping in long, slow motions over her burning flesh as he soothed away the sting of the crop. She inhaled his scent, a mix of brandy and male, coupled with the scent of arousal. Both hers and his.

It intoxicated her more than even the whip.

Roughly, her head was jerked back. "I asked you a question."

"Mmm-hmm," she barely managed. Her entire world had shifted, making it difficult to concentrate. His presence, the pain-tinged pleasure coursing through her and the impending act they would share pushed all coherence from her head.

She'd dared much more than she ever dreamed she would, but desperation drove her to it. Now, no matter the consequence, she was determined to have him, to share the ultimate act with the one man she did love. She would give him her virginity, however unknowingly he took it.

Matthew chuckled and pulled her upright and around. Reluctantly, Tori left the hard surface of the table, not fully ready to face him, despite her convictions and the luxuries he'd already taken with her body and the anonymity of the mask.

With her hands still bound behind her, Tori felt even more exposed as his gaze roamed over her. Like a physical touch, his dark blue eyes skimmed her body, from her nipple-hardened breasts all the way down the length of her bare legs, not missing an inch in between. She squirmed, leaning forward, anxious for his hands again. To feel him caress her with desire.

"Hmm, you please me, little one."

The words thrilled her. "I do?" she whispered, surprised and pleased at the same time.

"Yes." He tossed the crop to the table then reached out, slipping his fingers beneath the straps of her linen chemise. Slowly he skimmed her skin, drawing heat everywhere he touched. She looked down, watching his fingertips draw ever nearer to her breasts.

Oh God.

"Beautiful skin for a whore," he murmured, then frowned slightly, fingers stilling as he gripped the chemise. "Fine linen, too."

Fearing he was about to uncover her secret, Tori thrust her breasts upward and scrambled for a way to throw him off track. He would absolutely kill her if he discovered her identity. Suddenly, a passage from one of her most recent underground papers sprang into her head and she knew it was the perfect thing. Licking her lips, she lowered her eyes. "I had a very generous lover before he turned me out, sir. He took good care of me."

"Why did he cast you aside? Catch you with another man, hm?"

Tori shook her head wildly, not meeting his gaze. "No, of course not! I could never betray anyone."

Matthew remained silent, studying her for a moment before nodding. "His loss, little dove. I shall replace it for you."

His meaning was clear in the next moment as his strong hands ripped the material away, leaving her completely nude.

Tori gasped and instinctively tried to cover herself, but her bound hands prevented it.

Then she took note of the hungry, lustful look on Matthew's face and relaxed, feeling the power of her own body, realizing that while he controlled her, she could sway his actions. "Do you like, guv'nor?" she whispered, trying to interject the same light tone she'd heard the other girls use.

His smile was answer enough. He cupped one breast, lifting and testing the weight of her in his palm. She jerked in response.

"Interesting," he murmured, eyes locking with hers. When his thumb and forefinger encircled her hard nipple, Tori's lips parted, taken by the gentle touch.

"Are you sensitive here?" he asked.

"Yes," she replied.

The sensual, tender feeling escalated into pinpricks of pleasurable discomfort as he increased the pressure, squeezing her nipple hard. "Yes, what?"

She gasped for air and control, remembering his admonition not to spend. "Yes, yes, uh... oh, please."

"Yes, what?" he demanded again, tugging now, pulling her nipple away from her body with a steady force that took the weight of her breast with it.

Nearly unbearable desire battled unfamiliar pain and uncertainty. No man had ever touched her so.

"Ahh," she cried. "Sir, yes, sir."

"Tsk, tsk, you keep forgetting. I shall have to remedy that." Tipping his head, he regarded her steadily as he took command of her left breast and repeated the same movement until her back arched and tears formed at the corner of her eyes even as the pleasure intensified. She knew she would not last much longer, damn the consequences.

"Please, what?"

Tori licked her lips, breathing harshly through her mouth. "Oh," a sharp inhalation as he adjusted his grip. "Please, sir, may I come?"

Matthew let her breast fall and she nearly collapsed into the table. "No, I think not yet, little dove." He turned her around and removed the binding from her wrists. Gratefully, Tori rubbed the reddened flesh, wincing slightly as the blood rushed back in.

"Come here," he ordered, striding across the room, stopping before a large wingback chair.

Quickly she scurried forward. "Yes, sir?" Tori had to suppress a shiver just saying the words evoked. Always in her books she'd seen such things, had gotten excited by the reading of them and now to be saying them to him was enough to send her body past its limits. Her mind past its sanity.

"Undress me."

She froze, eyes flying up to his face, taking in the tautness of his lips, the hunger in his gaze. Suddenly realizing just how far he was going to take this, how far she would let him, Tori shivered with both fear and sexual excitement.

His hand swept out, catching her unprotected left buttock with a resounding crack. Squealing, she jumped, rubbing at the sting and glared at him. It took only seconds to recognize her error. Dropping both gaze and hands, she lowered her head.

"Please, sir, forgive me."

No sound, no movement came from Matthew, and Tori, loathe to look up again, kept her head dutifully bent, trying to calm her racing heart. Every salacious passage of her underground reading, every evocative recitation of her books that involved the joining of a man and woman flashed through her mind, sending jolts coursing through her as she imagined Matthew without clothing.

His hand descended heavily on the crown of her head, urging her down to her knees. "Release my cock," he commanded.

The mere words enflamed her and Tori very nearly spent then, but managed, barely, to maintain control. Hands shaking, she fumbled with the hidden fastening of his breeches, finally pulling the fabric apart enough to tug his white shirt out and away. He peeled it from his broad shoulders and tossed it aside. From her vantage point, Tori caught sight of his hard, rippled stomach and chest. His clothing hid so much from her eyes over the years. He was perfect to look at. Masculine, strong, far better than any fantasy she'd conjured.

The hair scattered over his body tapered between his nipples down the center of his body and into the waistband of his breeches, then beyond.

Suddenly, she wanted very much to follow that trail and tugged on his pants, pushing them over his muscular thighs, her palms lingering on his solid flesh, until the breeches puddled at his feet. Quickly stepping out, he kicked them away, now completely naked.

Tori remained frozen in her submissive position, staring for the first time at the sight of a man's cock, totally aroused. It looked much different than in her imagination. And no illustration from *The Opal* did it justice, either.

Long, dark and textured with veins, curly hair and an unmistakable scent of sex, it was the most beautifully intriguing thing she'd ever seen.

"God," she muttered involuntarily.

He laughed, his hands tangling in her hair once more. "Though you've not earned it, little dove, taste me."

As he forced her face closer to his crotch, Tori became aware of the heat emanating from him. Swirling, musky heat that enveloped her body and invaded her nostrils. She inhaled deeply, taking in his masculine aroma. Involuntarily, she licked her lips, eliciting a chuckle from him.

"Eager, aren't you? I like that." One final thrust at the back of her head and her lips met the head of his cock.

Tori's gasp of surprise allowed the velvety tip to penetrate her mouth, gliding effortlessly over her lips to lay heavily on her tongue. A hint of salt assailed her senses, the taste not unpleasant, but different. Holding her teeth open, she closed her eyes and tried to remember the ways her not-so-innocent literary adventuresses acted in this position. Tentatively, she compressed her lips around the thick shaft while lifting and trailing her tongue over the head.

He made a small noise and his fingers tightened in her hair.

"Deeper, dove, show me you know how to suck a cock."

He pistoned further than she was prepared for, the length of him intruding past her teeth and into her throat. She gagged and tried to pull away, but he wouldn't allow it.

"Come on, take it. Suck me."

Tori swallowed hard around his hot shaft and he groaned. With a start, she realized he liked it. And that she could breathe. Tightening her throat again produced the same reaction from him. Scooting into a more comfortable position on her knees, Tori edged closer, running her palms up his muscular, hair-dusted legs. Digging her fingernails into the tight flesh, she pulled him to her, delighted when her nose nuzzled the crisp hair above his cock.

"Christ," he muttered. "You are well-taught."

Tori eased backward, maintaining the hard suction and lubricating him with the spittle clinging to her tongue. Just as she reached the tip, her fingers encircled the base and she flicked in and out of the small hole before sliding down him again.

"Yes, just like that," he hissed, hands alternately fisting and relaxing in her hair.

Tori looked up, finding his head thrown back, Adam's apple working hard in his throat. His entire body was tense, as though he were on the verge of coming.

She smiled around her full mouth, knowing that for the moment, he might be the master, but she was the one in control. Putting herself wholeheartedly into the act, she re-doubled her efforts, determined to taste his spunk, whether he was ready to let it loose or not.

Matthew could not believe how good the dark haired nymphet was at sucking him. She'd had him near to the brink more than once and it took all his willpower to not spurt down her talented throat.

Despite the erotic high he rode, Matthew sensed the change in her from submissive maid to arrogant temptress. Immediately, he pulled his still hard cock from between her full lips and stepped backward, a frown on his face.

"I wasn't done," she pouted, gaze glittering sensually. Neither blue nor green, her eyes were an ever-changing mix of the two. The surrounding black lace of her mask helped shade them, making their color all the less visible.

He itched to remove her mask, but a gentleman's word was his honor and despite having all the power, he would tamp his curiosity for this night. Next time, he vowed, she would not hide from him.

"Get up."

Some of the smugness left her face and she rose, heavy breasts swaying.

"You've more than a hint of impertinence in you, dove. I must rectify that."

"Sir?" Her voice now contained a note of caution, exactly what he wanted.

"Spread your legs, hands behind your head."

Her hesitation lingered between them, ending only when he raised a brow and tipped his head. Finally, she complied, though she continued to hold his gaze. Oh yes, she was a delightful playmate. The right mix of submission and defiance, making the game all the more erotic.

Matthew walked around her, inspecting her much as he would a horse at Tattersall's. "Fine lines, you have, dove." He ran his hand over buttocks and down the back of her thigh, enjoying the quiver of her muscles beneath his palm.

"Wider," he ordered.

She complied, shuffling her feet apart on the carpet until the muscles of her inner thighs became taut.

Matthew slid his hand back up her leg, over the curve of her sweet bottom and through the cleft, chuckling as she gasped and leaned forward when his finger hesitated around the small, tight hole hidden there.

"Sir?" she questioned, voice high-pitched and definitely panic-stricken.

"Don't worry, dove, that will come eventually. But for now..."

He walked around to the front, looking down at her. Lips parted, eyes hazy, pulse beating a fevered pitch against her ivory skin. Matthew held her gaze as he encircled her small throat before turning his hand over and letting the backs of his fingers trail slowly down her chest, hovering at the plumpness of her breasts. He flicked at one and she inhaled. He smiled.

He continued over her ribs and down the slight swell of her belly.

She blinked rapidly, mouth opening and closing just as fast and he silently applauded her acting ability. She very nearly had him convinced she was a trembling maid, touched by a man for the first time.

She was a true artist.

He dipped down, lazily dragging his fingertips through her curly black pubic hair, spread his hand in a vee and pressed against her moist lips.

"Ah, what do we have here, little dove? Wet, are you?"

She didn't respond, her rosy mouth parted in anticipation.

Matthew closed his fingers, bringing her pussy lips together tightly, feeling her erect clit beneath the slippery skin.

She moaned softly.

He released her and tugged on a tuft of hair eliciting a small squeak of protest. "What is the rule?"

"I –,"

Her face held confusion, need and aggravation.

"Please, sir..."

"What is the rule?" he bit out, pulling harder.

She yelped, arms flying down to cover herself.

Matthew captured her wrists with his other hand and held them away. "Must I tie you again? I think so."

"No, please, sir, really, I won't do it again."

"Too late, little dove. You disobeyed me."

Her protests died when he turned her to the table once more, pushing her face down onto its wooden length. Settling himself between her legs, he splayed them until he caught her slight groan, then added an extra couple of inches. Using her ripped chemise, he bound her dainty ankles to the equally sleek legs of the table, giving her just enough room to shuffle, but not escape. Her hands he bound again with his cravat, behind her so her head and shoulders were thrust upward.

"Now then, little dove, what is the rule?"

No hesitation this time. "I must not spend until you allow it."

He nodded his approval and stroked his hands down her trembling back, over the curve of her buttocks and between her legs.

He found her wet, as he knew he would. She truly did enjoy it as much as he. Her obedience was fueled by her desires and he would ensure that she was well-rewarded.

But not just yet.

Matthew drew his forefinger through her dripping lips, spreading her juices over her stretched flesh. She shook at each movement, thrusting her hips as much as she could.

Her aroma was driving him mad. Sliding his finger into her wet hole, he stilled when she yelped, becoming stiff with what he nearly thought to be genuine fear. Dashing the notion, he wiggled his finger inside, withdrew it, then plunged back in. Her bottom swayed, but some of the tension left her shoulders and a soft mewling escaped her mouth.

Matthew added a second finger, marveling at the feel of her. She tightened and clenched, damn near tight as a virgin, but slick as a temptress. A high-pitched sound, much like a squeak escaped her and he pumped slow and long. Looking down, he marveled again at the satin texture and white sheen of her skin. His cock jumped with anticipation.

He leaned over her, nuzzling her ear as his fingers continued to fuck her. "For a whore, you're tight as a miser's purse."

She inhaled sharply and a fresh deluge of her passion coated his questing hand. "Do not spend, dove."

"I shan't, sir," she replied breathily.

"Do you feel how wet you are? How hot and grasping you are upon my fingers? How do you taste?"

She didn't respond, but small tremors continually shook her.

"Look at me," he said and withdrew his fingers. Glistening and heavy with her scent, he slid his tongue along one as she watched. Her audible gasp thrilled him.

"Never tasted yourself, dove?"

A small negative shake of her head was her only answer.

Matthew raised a brow and touched her lips with her juice-smeared finger. "It is high past time you did so. Open up."

Her eyes snapped at him in mulish disobedience and he frowned. "One last chance, pet, taste yourself or there will be no spending for you this night. I can, and will, torment you without release for your actions."

The threat worked. Tori squeezed her lids shut and opened her lips, taking his finger inside. She found herself pleasantly surprised at the taste. Sweet, yet a little salty. Much like him.

"Not so bad, is it? Mayhap another time we'll have one of the other girls join us," he murmured, withdrawing his finger.

"No!" she spit out, not caring whether he punished her or not, so great was her fury he would even suggest such a thing.

But rather than anger him, her swift denial seemed to amuse him. "We shall see. For now, I have plenty to handle with you."

He slipped his hand over her back again, causing her breath to hitch. Strong and determined, his fingers blazed a path down her spine and between the cleft of her bottom, hovering once more at the tight hole her cheeks covered. Involuntarily, she flinched.

Rubbing softly, he nipped her shoulder with his teeth, his lips close to her ear. "Has any man taken you here?"

"No, no sir."

His swift inhalation and the jerk of his still-hard cock against her thigh told her the confession aroused him greatly. "Please, no, sir, not there."

His finger traveled back to her dripping pussy, gathering the juices she knew still flowed from her. Tori relaxed slightly, relieved he was once more focused there. Until his now wet finger moved back up, pushing against the tight ring that refused him entrance.

Tori jerked away, but her bounds held tightly. "No," she whispered, mind and body whirling with conflicting needs. She could not allow this invasion, but the only way to stop it was reveal her identity. "Please do not."

Matthew's voice, low and dark, echoed in her ear. "Relax, little dove, just a bit of play this time. I will have your cunt this night, but next time..." He pushed a bit harder and she groaned as the tip of his finger slipped past the tight ring, filling her almost unbearably.

"Breathe," he commanded, moving his hand back and forth, his other dropping between her lower lips to find her clitoris. In moments the dual stimulation had her at the edge of orgasm.

Her lower body throbbed and hurt, as if gasping for air unsuccessfully. His fingers drew the pain deeper, turning it into a mindless pleasure that took over her senses and set her free. She was on the verge of spending when his voice filtered through her haze of need.

"You will not come."

The words jerked her back to the flat table, his insistent, intrusive hands and the tingles spanning her tits to toes. She groaned and swallowed, trying desperately to push away the need to climax, but it fought back.

"Please, sir," she begged, tipping her head to look back at him. "Please, I must, let me."

His hand dropped from her bottom to join the one at her cunt. He delved two fingers inside her, while tormenting her clit. "Oh God," she moaned, knowing now to resist was useless. He was pushing her over the edge intentionally.

Passion overcame reason and she keened wildly, pushing back at him fucking herself on his fingers, loving the stretch, the invasion, the pounding need.

He slowed his rhythm as she came, until his thumb alone stroked at her clitoris.

Tori realized almost immediately that more trouble was in store for her this night.

She also found she couldn't wait to experience it.

Slowly, Matthew withdrew from the limp, heaving, glorious body of the whore still bound to the table. It took every ounce of control, plus some he didn't know he had, not to impale her wide open cunt with his very hard cock.

But at last he'd found a willing, knowing playmate who took his punishments, his domination with exactly the right mix of obedience and defiance. Ripe, wanton and eager, this girl, and her delectable form, would serve him well again and again. He needed to pace himself before taking her.

If he could restrain himself. Moodily, Matthew spun away, leaving her still moaning, twitching and tied, heading for the well-stocked bar Lizzeth kept for him. Pouring a draught of cheap brandy, he studied the raven-haired harlot and contemplated his next move. The liquor he'd already consumed, coupled with the knock-off rot gut he sipped at now would undoubtedly keep any orgasm of his at bay. The notion of taking her now, while she remained stunned and utterly helpless, appealed greatly.

A familiar, demanding twitch from his crotch echoed the sentiment. Slugging back the last of the bitter brandy, Matthew set the glass aside, strode behind her and grabbed a fistful of her hair, lightly yanking her upward.

She shrieked, obviously still in a state of orgasmic euphoria.

"I told you not to come, didn't I, little bitch? You'll pay for that, but for now..."

Without further warning or ado, Matthew fitted the head of his cock to her still slick lower lips and sank in.

The whore became almost unnaturally still and for a moment Matthew sobered, fearing he may have gone too far, too quickly. But a shake of her head, the hitch of her breath and a soft, nearly imperceptible moan compelled him forward.

Yanking harder on her hair, he muttered low, filthy words to her, finding each verbal assault tightened her muscles around him. Her body, intent on resisting him, clenched and pushed back as if trying to force him back out.

Matthew chuckled, once more reassured this one knew the game as well, if not better, than he. After all, her ingénue act of innocence was dead on, belied only by the skill of her whore's body.

A very tight body. Concentrating now on winning this battle, Matthew shoved his hips forward, sinking further into her, ripping a squealing gasp from her throat. Another push, another half-protesting squeak.

Then suddenly, like the lighting of a torch he broke her, his stiff cock surging ahead into her dripping pussy, settling deep within her tightness.

She groaned again and once more she stilled, back bowed by the grip of his hand in her hair and the invading cock riding her lower body. The pain was immense, sucking both her breath and her senses until all she could see was a pinpoint of light behind her tightly squeezed eyes. Tori whimpered as the throbbing, deep-seated invader moved backward, drawing her pain out with it. Relaxing minutely, she gulped desperate to regain control, until he slid inside again. She groaned at the tenderness his cock served up as it slid easily into her tightness.

Back again, slowly, the joining of their bodies eased by the copious amounts of desire he'd wrenched from her. In.

Matthew pulled on her hair and she arched backward, shifting her hips out of necessity and emitted another mewl of surprise as he slipped further inside. The surprise came with the realization she no longer hurt. The tenderness, coupled with the heat of his thrusting cock, served to highlight the pinpricks of desire coursing through her once more. When his hand dropped from her hair and found her clitoris, she was completely lost.

Her entire being focused on the ascending spiral, the approaching orgasm he was skillfully coaxing from her. "Please." The word slipped from her mouth, almost of its own volition.

He chuckled and landed a light slap to her flank, thrusting harder. "Please what, little slut?"

The uncontrollable clenching of her pussy told them both how much his words, and his actions, affected her. Another slap.

"Please what?"

"God, please, I, may I, oh..." the words trailed away as he left off her clitoris, grabbed both of her lower lips and ground himself inside as far as he could go. She'd never experienced anything like it. Again, thrown off her axis, she concentrated only on the incredibly wonderful feelings he'd stoked. "Yes, please, yes, like that."

He stopped all motion, held so deep inside her that she could feel every pulse of his heartbeat in the rigid length of his hard cock. "Do not come until I give you permission."

She groaned, but nodded, needing both the release and the permission now more than ever.

He pulled back, stretching her lips and thighs just a bit further then pistoned his hips back and forth, titillating every nerve in her body. Tori clenched her fists, fighting back the building orgasm until at last she feared she would burst without it.

"Please, sir, oh please, I beg you, let me come."

She squeezed her inner muscles, frantically attempting to get him to spend so that she could as well.

Matthew stiffened behind her, released her nether lips and grabbed her bottom, slamming hard and deep within her. "Curse your talented pussy, minx."

The heat, the pace of his thrusts, the words took her over the edge and she came endlessly, the word please still tumbling pell mell from her lips.

He groaned and lodged himself against the cleft of her ass. She felt each spurt of his spunk as he jetted his release. It set off another round of orgasm for her until she lay on the tabletop, a quivering mass of unbridled nerve endings.

Matthew pulled out of the girl's tight, talented body and, on shaking legs, grabbed a nearby towel, wiping himself clean. With dazed eyes, he watched her trembling form, knowing if her equally compelling mouth wrapped around him to clean their combined juices, he'd be spurting again like a schoolboy. And he had far better plans for the vixen this night than to waste another load so soon.

With a raspy laugh, he tossed the towel aside, unbound her and helped her up. He stilled for a moment, enveloped in an almost-familiar fragrance of lavender and roses, but before he could think on it further, he noticed her mask was slightly askew. It revealed the high, sweet curve of a cheekbone and just the outer edge of one eye. Quickly, her hands flew up and adjusted the concealing headdress. If not for his gentlemanly bond, he'd ripped the damn thing from her and feast upon the loveliness he somehow knew he'd find beneath it.

Instead, he chucked her under the chin like a chit, then turned and strode to the bar. "A brandy before we begin again?"

"Again?" she squeaked.

Matthew turned, half-smiling. "Of course, little dove. I've paid for the entire night and I intend to use your delicious, obedient body every way I want."

Tori licked her lips as panic assailed her. One or two hours out of the house she could manage, but all night? She would be doomed to a cloister, never mind the wholly repugnant thought of marriage to the elderly colonel. She paused, thinking hard. A convent, she decided, would be the far more appealing life.

"I'd love a brandy, sir," she replied, licking her lips.

Chapter Four

TORI CREPT UP THE BACK alleyway toward her house on trembling legs, eyes gritty from lack of sleep, body sore, aware, and vibrantly alive.

Though she hated sneaking away from Matthew as he slept, she could not risk exposing her identity. She did not regret a single moment of their illicit night and it only served to further her determination to wed him. A marriage without Matthew would be one doomed to no passion, no desire, no love.

She would not settle for that.

The sun peeked over the trees and the city stirred as it woke, telling her she must find her bed and soon if she wished to avoid discovery.

She swung the door open noiselessly. A few short steps and she mounted the staircase, passing no one. Praying her luck would continue to hold, Tori snuck into her room and quietly closed the door behind her, turning the key with shaking fingers.

She'd done it, by God. Unbelievable. The entire night from the party to the encounter on the balcony to the erotic sex she'd shared with Matthew. All done without being caught. Laurel would never believe her.

Tori struggled from her dress, ruing the ruined chemise. Crumpling it into a ball, she shoved it into the depths of the wardrobe to dispose of later.

Taking in her naked appearance in the looking glass, she gasped, running fingers over the light welts left by his crop. Her thighs and bottom bore the brunt of the strokes, thankfully areas no one save herself would see. They would heal and disappear, leaving her only with the delicious, erotic memories of their making.

Slipping her nightdress on, Tori climbed into bed, flopping on her back with a groan. Three hours would not be nearly enough rest, but it would have to suffice.

Once the matter of the blackmailer was over and done with, she would redouble her efforts to seduce Matthew into marriage.

MATTHEW STRODE INTO his townhouse, brushing past Stires and made for the study. Fury fueled his every step. Waking alone had been bad enough, finding out he'd been duped even worse.

To learn the woman he'd so sensuously tortured was a member of his own class, a woman who paid to take the place of a whore, infuriated him.

Just one more reason his mistrust in women was so well-placed.

He would find the deceitful bitch. He would find her and make her rue what she'd dared.

"Food," he snapped at the hovering butler. "Have water heated for a bath and lay out some new clothes."

"Yes, sir."

"I've several stops to make, so ready the carriage."

Stires nodded and drew the doors closed, only to open them a moment later. "Sir, if I may be so bold. Are you well?"

Matthew stood rigid in front of his desk, staring with unseeing eyes at the crumpled half-mask he held. The only reminder she'd left behind.

Well? Hell no, he was not well. He'd found the woman of his dreams in a brothel only to find he'd been played the fool.

Again.

Sick to his stomach at the implications and the possibilities, Matthew drummed his fingers on the leather-covered mahogany desktop.

"I will be fine, Stires."

The deep silence told him his longtime butler didn't believe him, with good reason.

"Very good, my lord," Stires said stiffly and retired from the room.

Matthew shrugged from his coat and flung it to the divan, relieving only a minimal bit of his pent-up fury.

He reached for the brandy decanter then pulled back. He would need all of his faculties sharp and alert. Settling into his desk, he scratched out some notes of what he remembered about her. Which was damn near everything, right down to the small mole on the right side of her hip, just above the bone.

Long dark hair. Slight frame. Her eyes were various shades of blue-green, depending on her level of excitement. When she came, they turned the most incredible shade of jade.

Despite his anger, his cock stirred. She'd been his every desire, fulfilled his requests and took his cock and his whip with equal fervor.

Ripping his wandering mind away from the memories, he stared down at his list and cursed aloud.

Half the women of the Ton fit her description.

Bloody hell, why had he allowed her to keep the mask on? Feeling even more the idiot, he realized the covering was her way of ensuring her identity remained hidden. She played upon his honor by demanding his word as a gentleman to keep it intact.

How many whores would even think of such a thing?

Stires reappeared with his breakfast. "Your bath shall be ready soon, my lord."

Matthew nodded, waving him away.

There'd been something about the way she spoke, the way her mouth moved.

Christ, he couldn't concentrate on that because all he saw were her lips wrapped around him.

Stires returned. "Lord Ashford, my lord. Will you see him?"

"'Course he will, man, have you lost all your senses?"

Ryder strode into the room and gave the butler an odd look before passing it on to Matthew. "What the deuce is bedeviling you?"

Matthew spooned eggs into his mouth and avoided an answer. Knowing his friend's insatiable curiosity, Ryder would gladly take up the hunt with him. But Matthew found he wanted that pleasure all to himself.

Equal parts anger mixed with fascination. Anticipation. No, he alone would hunt his lady in whore's clothing.

"Long night," he finally murmured and waved a hand to a chair. "Sit down. Breakfast?"

"No," Ryder replied. "I just stopped by to invite you to Thursday night dinner."

Matthew cocked a brow. "A dinner invitation that warrants a personal visit? And four days in advance? What's the occasion?" Then it hit him and the eggs soured in his stomach. "Tori's engagement dinner?"

Ryder's jaw clenched. "If my mother had her way it would be. But no, not quite yet."

Son of a bitch. Matthew dragged in a lungful of air and contemplated his friend. Mayhap he should reconsider that brandy. "I take it you do not agree with the prospective nuptials?"

"I have no reason to dispute them."

"But?"

Ryder shrugged. "He's older than Mother. A stodgy fool like the Colonel will break Tori's spirit. It is not the life I would have for her. She needs someone younger, someone who will love her."

Matthew snorted. "Love is a ridiculously over-admired commodity, Ashford. It does not exist."

"You thought it did once."

"And I was a fool proven wrong many times over." Gripping his fork tightly, he fought for calm. He didn't like the idea of Tori marrying the aging army man any more than Ryder, but it was her choice. "She'll be fine, that one. Lands on her feet all the time. 'Sides, she can always shoot him if he mistreats her."

Ryder's scowl remained for a moment longer then he sighed with a rueful grin. "Suppose I ought to gift her with a new lady's gun just in case there's a wedding."

Matthew nodded. "Excellent idea."

"Right then. So, you will come to the dinner?"

He didn't want to go, he wanted to hunt. To seek the woman haunting his body, his mind. But he could not desert Ashford or Tori. "I'll be there."

"YOU ARE VERY QUIET, Miss Ashford."

The Colonel's voice held a note of censure he obviously did not mean to disguise.

Tori turned to face him, gripping the reins tighter. "You sound disapproving."

"Merely confused. You are usually such a vivacious, effusive woman. Always smiling or laughing. You've done neither the entire morning."

Tori blinked at his accurate assessment. She'd been deeply contemplative – one might say quite worried – since her blackmailer failed to show two hours earlier. No note, no ribbon, no meeting. She was most definitely on edge. "Odd that you would know something like that Colonel, when I have only just made your acquaintance."

He shrugged. "I have had my eye on you for some time, Miss Ashford."

A chill skittered over her. "Oh?"

He laughed, mustache wiggling vigorously. "Calm yourself, my dear. You are a very beautiful woman and I have been drawn to you at the various gatherings we've both attended. It was not until recently that I shored up the nerve to approach you."

Tori relaxed, comforted by the laughter in his gaze. Feeling the fool for seeing shadows when none existed, she straightened in the saddle and mustered a smile. "No apologies required, Colonel."

He edged his mount closer. "I ah, I had hoped you would be receptive to my suit."

Good humor fled in a wink. Her newfound knowledge precluded any sort of sham marriage, especially one to such an old man. Holding fast to her hope of being only with Matthew, she cleared her throat. "Um, Colonel, I am flattered, of course, but..."

She trailed off, noting the darkness gathering in his eyes, the strain of anger now visible on his face. The man shifted moods faster than any female of her acquaintance. Not that she needed it, but the observation was another notch against him.

"But?" he prompted, voice harsh.

"But," she plowed on, "I do not believe we will suit. You will be much better off with someone a bit–" Tori struggled for the right word, discarding *older* out of hand. She did not wish to injure his pride any more than necessary. "Someone more experienced than I."

The Colonel reached out and grabbed her horse's halter, forcing them both to a stop. Tori froze, eyes wide and heart racing. Surely he would not dare anything improper here. Already she caught a few interested glances tossed their way by other riders in the park.

Oh, dear. Mayhap she should have said older after all.

"What I require, Miss Ashford, is your obedience in this matter. You will gain the necessary experience, I will see to that."

Again, what should have sounded innocuous instead bore the stamp of threat. Tori swallowed hard. "We should return, my mother will worry over me."

The Colonel shook his head. "She knows I will take care of you."

More panic assailed her and Tori drew herself up. "Colonel Jameson, I feel a touch of stomachache coming on and unless you would care for me to retch over your polished boots, I suggest you take me home. Now."

The war of wills continued in silence for another tense moment. Tori really did think she might lose her breakfast on him, but finally he nodded, the anger seeping away.

The man was more mercurial than the London weather.

"Of course, my dear, I apologize. Let us return and I will call on you tomorrow to discuss our future."

He turned the horses and headed back through Hyde Park while Tori reeled at his high-handed assumption. But she remained silent, not willing to rouse his temper once more.

Colonel Jameson frightened her. Not many men had that ability, especially since her brother and Matthew schooled her quite adeptly in the use of pistols.

When at last they reached the townhouse, she dismounted quickly.

"Good day, Colonel." Sketching out the briefest of curtsies, she gathered her skirts and darted inside. To her dismay, he followed her.

"Miss Ashford, a moment, please."

Slowly she faced him. "Yes?"

His blue eyes traveled the length of her body and he tapped his riding crop along his leg. Unlike the night before when Matthew wielded the same instrument with lascivious delight, the Colonel's handling of it made her uneasy. His gruff voice was unyielding when he addressed her. "When we are wed, you will be more docile."

His audacity astounded her. To bloody hell with his feelings, she would not stand for such remarks. "Then it is a good thing we are not to be married, Colonel. I trust you will understand when I tell you I do not wish to see you again."

He chuckled, the crop moving faster. "And I hope *you* understand when I tell you the decision is no longer yours to make. I have struck a bargain with your mother, Miss Ashford. Tell her I extend my regards to our mutual friend Mr. Wolffe." The Colonel leaned forward, the look in his eyes chilling and hard. "I look forward to relieving you of your arrogance along with your innocence. Good day."

Turning sharply on the heel of his boot, he sauntered out the door, leaving Tori speechless, infuriated and more frightened than ever. What the deuce was going on? What bargain?

It took quite a feat, but she finally managed to gain control of herself, thanking prudence no firearm was readily available and set off in search of her mother.

She found her seated comfortably on a settee, sewing basket at her side, head bent over her stitching.

"Mother," Tori said sharply, "why is the Colonel so positive I'm going to marry him?"

Her mother jumped and exclaimed, lifting her finger to her mouth. "Victoria, a lady should be demure and quiet, not bellowing about like a sailor."

Tori ignored the admonition. "Why?"

Lady Ashford sighed and put the sewing away, patting the chaise. "Come sit and cease your hysterics."

Sinking down, she eyed her mother warily. "He has a high opinion of himself and he speaks out of turn."

"As do most of the young bucks in Town." Her mother rubbed the top of her hand and for the first time Tori noticed the dark blue veins so prominently evident. She was always so forceful it never occurred to her she could be growing old.

"Would it truly be so horrible, being married to him? Your future would be secure. Your children will never want."

"But *I* would, Mama, I would."

"You promised me you would give him a chance."

Tori debated sharing the shocking statement about her innocence he'd made. Instead, she picked at the feather adorning her riding hat. "Aye, that is true enough and I have, don't you think?"

"No, I do not." Mama softened her expression. "Darling, would it be too much to ask for some enthusiasm? He is not a leper, you know. Trust me, Victoria. I would do you no harm."

"I know that, Mama." Tori wasn't entirely sure she believed the sentiment, though. "But why him? Why now? The Season is not even half over."

"Victoria, please." Her mother gave her a wan smile, though her mouth was tight. "He's a good man, he deserves a fair chance. Now, go upstairs, dear, and rest a bit." She cleared her throat as she picked her sewing up once more. "I have arranged a party for Thursday night. Just family and few close friends. Laurel, of course. And the Colonel."

Tori gave a sigh of her own. Wonderful, one more quandary from which to extricate herself. She rose and started from the room, stopping only when she reached the doorway, a sudden question on her lips. "Mother?"

"Yes?"

"Who is this Mr. Wolffe?"

The countess whitened visibly and swayed, catching the back of the chaise with one hand, the other flying to her mouth. "What?" she whispered, eyes wide. "What did you say?"

Tori blinked several times, unease tingling down her spine. Something was very amiss. "Mr. Wolffe. The Colonel mentioned him again. Who is he?"

"Bloody hell."

Tori could not believe she'd heard her mother utter the blasphemous words, but she was pretty darn certain she had.

Lady Ashford crossed the room rapidly. "What did he say about him?" her mother asked, though oddly no hint of her anxiety now remained.

"I, uh, nothing, really," Tori stammered. "Just to pass along his greetings."

"You're certain that's all?"

"Yes." What on earth was going on? Tori felt bewildered, completely off-kilter. Corwin, the blackmailer, the Colonel, her mother's odd behavior. It was all very nearly too much to take in. "You're not going to tell me, are you?"

Mother's gaze flicked away for a moment before meeting her stare head on. "Trust me when I say he is of no importance. I do not know why the Colonel continues to mention him. Why I don't think I've even seen the man more than once. Quite peculiar." She tipped her head. "And you're certain he didn't say anything? No clue as to who this Mr. Wolffe is?

"No, I, I just assumed you knew and there was, oh I don't know. I'm quite confused at the moment."

Her mother's smile softened. "Go on, sweetling, upstairs and rest. You'll feel right as rain, soon."

Tori nodded, mind whirling, trying to decipher just what her mother wasn't saying. Because Tori knew she was hiding something. She recognized the signs. "Yes, of course. I shall go upstairs, to rest." Tori fled to her room, aware of her mother's sharp gaze on her back. She must sort all of this out and quickly before anymore unforeseen drama occurred.

But really, who was this mysterious Mr. Wolffe? And why was Mother so keen on avoiding anything discussion about him at all. Perhaps her brother would know. And while she was questioning him, she would make it a point to apprise him of her distaste for the Colonel's suit.

She'd just gained the landing upstairs when Glory caught up with her.

"These have just arrived for you, Miss Ashford." The maid gave over two crisply pressed parchments.

Tori took them pleased her hand did not shake and betray her onset of nerves. One bore a close resemblance to the previous blackmail note; the other she recognized as a message from the editor of *The Opal.* "When did these arrive?"

"Boy brought them 'round back just now, Miss," Glory replied.

"The notes arrived together?"

"Aye."

"Thank you." Tori nodded and turned away. She wasn't entirely certain how messenger boys worked or if there was a system, a territory, or something of the sort, but unease rippled through her at the notion these two notes arrived for her at the same time.

"No, surely a coincidence, nothing more." Flipping the envelopes over, she noted with great relief the seals were intact. "There, nothing to fret over." Tori debated sending for Laurel, thought better of it and retreated to her room. The time for pussyfooting was long past.

Securing the lock, she carried the notes to her writing desk and breath held, prayers muttered, broke the wax on the blackmail note.

Miss Ashford,

My apologies for missing you this morning, I was unavoidably detained. I will contact you again soon. Be waiting.

~Fondest regards.

"Regards, my left foot." Tori read and re-read the note, seeking any clue to the writer's identity, finding none, of course.

Head aching from trying to make sense where none could be found, she re-folded the paper closed, stuffing it into a cranny of her desk.

Picking up the other message, she found a coded note from her editor requesting a certain type of story. One featuring beautiful young women at the mercy of an alluring, dangerous man. Her newfound knowledge would certainly assist her with the writing.

And the sum the editor offered was quite enough to refill her coffers of the one hundred pounds demanded by her blackmailer. Eventually.

She sighed, head still pounding. Perhaps she could take her earnings and flee to the continent for a time. Greece or Rome, even. But that would mean leaving Matthew.

"This is getting me nowhere," she muttered, rubbing her temple. Digging for clean paper, she tried to accommodate her editor. Odd thing was, every scene, every bit of dialogue she wrote seemed too vague, not delving deep enough into the reality of the experience of submitting to a masterful man.

Nodding, she scribbled a few of the more exotic memories of her night with Matthew, adding more and more detail until she had to stop and relieve herself of the pent-up need.

Her pussy pounded terribly, her lower lips swollen and throbbing with a deep ache. Her rapid heartbeat pulsed, causing the thrum to stoke her higher. Doffing her riding habit and chemise, Tori stretched out on her bed, clad only in her silk stockings, spread her legs and slid her fingertips along the upper edges of her thigh.

Around and down the outside of her pussy, she teased herself. Her other palm skimmed along her belly, catching the soft mound of her left breast, tweaking the hard nipple between forefinger and thumb. She moaned at the tightness, the tingle of pleasurable pain.

Nothing so great as the sweet torture inflicted by Matthew, but enough to push her higher to orgasm.

Tori spread her slick lips wide, arching her hips, breath hitching as the air hit her sensitive clit. Falling back down, she rubbed her thumb over the swollen flesh, slipping one long finger inside herself, marveling at the wetness, the way she grasped and tightened.

Was this how Matthew felt when his cock slid into her? Had the muscles of her cunt gripped him with this much heat and demand?

She stroked the finger in and out, moving her other hand down to continue toying with her clit, mimicking his movements, wishing he were with her. Holding her, whispering to her with low words of need.

Tori moaned, head thrashing as the pulsating grew stronger, harsher. Matthew beside her. Inside her. Stoking her. Only he could bring this out in her, only he could quench the fire.

Closer she drew, gasping for breath now, eyes tightly clenched, legs stiff.

"Matthew," she murmured, picturing him as he'd been at the last – poised above her, muscled arms straining with his weight as he slid slow and deep into her body, each movement controlled and timed for the ultimate response. He'd held her eyes, staring so intently she almost feared he knew.

Instead his hips plunged, his face contorted and he yelled as his cock throbbed inside her.

It was in that moment she knew she was his forever. There would never be another man for her.

Matthew. His name coupled with the magic of her own questing fingers threw her over the edge and she orgasmed. A long, delicious spasm that wracked her body, while her empty soul cried for him.

MATTHEW DOWNED HIS third glass of champagne, letting his eyes scan the crush of people, skipping over those women who could not be his submissive miss. Past the blondes, those with blue eyes and the tall girls who stood with awkward hope near overbearing chaperones.

No, none of them could have engineered and carried out a plan of such daring as his mystery woman. Though eager to obey, he'd detected a core of strength inside her. Outside the bedroom, he doubted she would bend quite so easily.

Of course, his observations now did him little good. He could not find her and his odd rash of appearances at nearly every ball, fete and recital in town had caused a stir of excitement through the rushes of

Marrying Mamas these past three days. He found himself under intense scrutiny and it irritated him almost as much as being played the fool.

Almost.

A passing waiter offered another glass, but Matthew refused it, noting the time was much later than he anticipated. He must put aside his hunt for the moment and make for the Ashford townhouse.

Climbing into his carriage, he slumped against the back, stretched his legs out and rubbed his brow, pondering once more the possible identity of his prey.

He'd come to the conclusion tonight that no young thing seeking a husband would dare such an act no matter the bravado she carried. The decision to eliminate those debutantes pleased him as he could not stomach the thought of having been made the fool by a young, virginal chit out for a lark.

That left the bevy of widows – the women who enjoyed the freedom of their late husband's estates and the allowances given them by society in regards to their liaisons. He decided he should also include the dallying marrieds of his acquaintance. Boredom oft drove a woman to desperate deeds.

But who among his female peers would commit such an audacious act? And why him?

That question plagued him constantly. He knew he'd been chosen specifically, the whore at Lizzeth's confirmed that much. Requested him by name and description. But why?

A woman who sought his attention, but lacked the nerve to approach him directly?

A still married woman seeking a bit of excitement outside her own marriage bed?

Both were plausible, but damned if he knew which was true.

For one horrifying moment, he'd even wondered if the mystery woman was his ex-fiancée. Now that was a truth he could not have borne. Cecily had come back once after his brother died and Matthew inherited the earldom. As beautiful and deceitful as ever, widowed and begging his forgiveness. He'd felt no emotion turning her away, banishing her once more from his life.

The carriage rumbled to a swaying stop and the door popped open. Climbing down, Matthew tugged his sleeves, straightened his cravat and headed up the walk to pound the brass knocker.

"Corwin, 'bout damn time," Ryder grumbled as he answered the summons. "Mother and Victoria have been going 'round and 'round about serving dinner, waiting for you."

Matthew smiled. "Why are you answering the door? Who won?"

"Happened to be passing by when you arrived. Tori."

He clapped his friend on the shoulder. "Then let us proceed to the table, lest your mother decides we should have our eyes blackened for further delaying her meal."

The company gathered in the drawing room stood at their entrance and introductions swiftly ensued among the party of ten. Lady Ashford spared him a sharp glare before leading everyone to the dining room escorted by the Duke of Grafton.

Scanning the table, he quickly found his place card, not overly surprised to find himself seated next to the grand dame herself. The woman was shrewd. Seating him next to her, she'd placed Tori between Ryder and the Colonel at the opposite end of the table. The other guests filled the remaining seats, alternating male to female as was the norm.

Matthew chafed at finding himself seated too far away from Tori to achieve any sort of discreet conversation.

He could not believe she seriously entertained the notion of marriage with the ex-Army man. He looked down the table at the Colonel, staring at the older man with harsh scrutiny. As if sensing his regard, the Colonel turned and met his stare, mustache bristling, brow raised.

Pointedly, Matthew swung his gaze to Tori then back to the Colonel and let his opinion clearly be made. The older man stiffened, neck and ears reddening, hand balling into a fist.

"Corwin, start a fight at my table and you will find yourself on the first ship to the Americas," Lady Ashford's soft, yet unyielding voice sounded in his ear.

He nodded shortly. "I would dream of no such act, Lady Ashford. It is a night meant for merry-making, is it not? One meant to secure Victoria's future?"

Lady Ashford's lips twitched, reminding him oddly of the Colonel's mustache. "That is not your concern, Corwin. Behave in a fashion worthy of your station."

She shifted in her chair, turning away to speak to someone else and Matthew found himself gripping his fork with great force.

Not his concern.

But she was. Had been for quite some time. Hell, Tori wormed her way into his fantasies more often than he found comfortable, but the pleasurable outcome always outweighed the slight guilt.

He cast a look down the table at her as she chatted with her friend Laurel. Tori wore her dark hair swept up, coiled and curled to set off the elegant length of her neck and strong line of her jaw. She wore a gown of deep green, which matched her eyes.

She laughed, mouth pursing with delight at something Laurel said. Matthew blinked focusing his gaze on her lips. Full and red, he could still remember exactly how she'd tasted.

Tori sipped at her drink, tongue slipping out to catch a stray drop of champagne and Matthew nearly groaned aloud.

A woman like her could very nearly change his mind about marriage. But it was not for him. One near-marriage to a member of the lying sex was plenty for him. No, he'd take his pleasures as he had been – by assignation, gold coin and chance.

Tori laughed, a deep throaty sound that pulled his eyes back to her. She leaned forward and he lost her behind the centerpiece, a towering bouquet of white roses and baby's breath.

When she sat back again, she was shaking her head and merriment gleamed from her. He smiled in response, thinking she looked like nothing so much as a mischievous imp. A swathe of curls escaped one of the pins and fell forward, covering her cheek.

Matthew froze, staring at her half-hidden features.

Impossible.

The air in the room suddenly seemed thick and harsh, and he, unable to breathe it in. Lightheaded, dizzy and disbelieving, Matthew continued to look at her.

With every passing moment the truth became more evident. The hair, the skin, the eyes, her delightfully talented mouth.

He groaned.

"Are you all right, Corwin?" Ashford spoke from the head of the table.

With effort, Matthew pulled his gaze away from Tori. "I'm fine," he gritted out, the lie coming easily. His rational side argued he was mistaken. Tori could never have engaged in the wanton activities he'd shared with the mystery woman.

She was but a girl, had no knowledge of anything remotely sexual, much less the adventurous romp he'd enjoyed with his anonymous bed partner.

And my God, she would have been a virgin!

"Lord Sussex, are you unwell, sir?"

Tori's soft voice intruded on his private argument.

Sir. His cock stiffened at the sweet sound and he knew for certain then. The treacherous bitch he hunted was none other than Victoria Rose Ashford.

Slowly, he raised his head, meeting her concerned look head on. A muscle ticked in his jaw from the effort he engaged to remain civil.

'twas not possible. Tori was the one woman he knew would never betray him, who held no deceit in her bones, the one he could always trust. But he could not doubt the proof before him.

The table grew silent and he felt the weight of everyone's attention.

Tori's eyes widened and a rosy hue crested her cheeks. She bit her lip and his hand fisted in reaction.

With measured, precise calm, he placed his napkin on the table, stood and bowed to Lady Ashford. "Please forgive my unseemly exit, but I am suddenly feeling quite ill."

He heard Ryder's muffled snort as his mother glanced quickly at the food.

"Rest assured, madame, it is an affliction I believe I incurred a few nights ago and not anything to do with your fine feast."

Tori's low gasp caught his ear and he turned to look at her again, having managed to shroud his fury for the moment.

Lifting his glass, he quirked a brow at her. "I find it best I retire to my own house so as not to *condemn* any of you to this illness." He caught Tori's wince at his deliberate verbal jab. She knew he'd unmasked her. Her obvious guilt further provoked his anger. "Before I depart however, I would like to make a toast. To Miss Ashford. May you have a lifetime of happiness, bereft of deception and betrayal."

Everyone save he and Tori sipped to the odd toast, murmuring low words of assent. He noted the tears forming in her eyes, saw her half-rise from the chair.

"Thank you for your *kind* words, my lord. Please, allow me to walk you to the door?"

The Colonel harrumphed and she spared not a glance for him. Didn't give a damn what anyone else in the room – brother or prospective intended – thought of it, Matthew supposed, a reluctant spark of admiration popping into his very irrational thoughts.

"No," Matthew replied, waving her back down. "Least of all you." He paused, knowing she sensed his displeasure, his anger. "It would not do for you to become ill, as well."

"Quite right, Corwin." Lady Ashford smiled.

He bowed to the room at large, turned and left, pace quickening with every step he took toward the door. Away from her.

Slamming into his carriage, he threw himself against the cushioned bench, seething. His pride demanded action, the retaliation he'd so carefully crafted.

But not now. Now, he only wanted to return to the sanctuary of his home and come to terms with the truth.

Tori had betrayed him.

Chapter Five

WITH BACK-ALLEY SKILLS learned at university, Matthew climbed a well-placed tree outside Tori's window, eased the sash up and dropped inside. The soft whisper of her breath sounded from his left and he turned his head, finding her bed. He grinned as the rising posters distinguished themselves in the night.

Perfect.

He rose, closed the window and doffed his hat and jacket. Silently he set his bag of carefully selected implements on the floor. He crossed the room, felt for the door handle and turned the key, then pocketed it.

He had trapped his lady-whore. And tonight, she would pay for her betrayal.

Matthew struck a flint and lit the lamp on her writing desk. The golden glow spread across the papers on the surface and he paused, catching sight of a familiar looking bit of parchment just peeking out from a nook in the desk.

More lies, more proof she was not the innocent he thought. Picking up the latest edition of *The Opal Chronicles*, he crumpled it in his fist. Her deception defied description and this discovery fueled his displeasure even more. How could she have done this to him?

She stirred behind him and Matthew tossed the paper down then crossed to her bedside on quick, silent feet.

He inhaled sharply, suddenly fighting the urge to wake her with a kiss that started out tenderly and quickly heated into a passion that he knew she matched. Asleep on her back, her dark hair spread out in a silken wave, tempting him to wrap his hands in it as he'd done three nights earlier. She'd liked that, had begged for her.

Matthew gave himself a mental shake, raking his gaze over her slumbering form. When his dark eyes returned to her sweet, pointed face, he found it marred by a frown.

Good, obviously her guilt-ridden mind gave her no ease.

Now he would mete out his own justice. Drawing a length of black silk from his pocket, he leaned down and settled his hand over her mouth.

Immediately her eyes popped open and she fought him. Matthew grunted, impressed by her strength – her slight frame belied hidden abilities.

"Cease your struggles," he hissed, pressing his face closer. It was a mistake. Her scent, a combination of lavender and feminine musk, invaded his senses. The softness of her lips beneath his palm further dismayed him. He remembered all of it from the night they'd spent together.

Why hadn't he known her then?

"Be still Victoria," he muttered again and she finally ceased, eyes widening as she appeared to recognize him at last. Her body softened, though he still read fear in her green eyes.

The rage that had spurred him from the moment of discovery suddenly evaporated, leaving only a dark need to exact revenge.

Her sensual torture was just about to begin.

Tori's lips moved and he shook his head. "Not a word from you this night unless I command it."

He lifted his hand and she opened her mouth. "No," he barked, dangling the silk in front of her. "Unless you wish to be gagged as well as restrained?"

She shook her head and remained silent. Matthew lifted his palm away. Her tongue slid along her lips and his breath hitched as more memories and new ideas peppered him.

He grunted, knowing he would put that tongue to good use tonight.

Pulling the bedclothes from her, he swept his gaze over her form, almost laughing at her modest covering. The heavy nightdress did nothing to hide the pebbling of her nipples or the womanly spread of her hips.

"Matthew," she breathed, arms reaching up for him.

"Ah, ah, ah," he said, straddling her hips. Grabbing hold of her arms, he tugged them up and outward, securing each to a bedpost. She tensed, but remained silent.

With a light touch, he pulled his fingertips down her bound wrists and arms, absorbing the exquisite touch of her tender flesh beneath her gown. Supple and firm, he wanted to run his mouth along every inch of her, taste her once more.

His cock stiffened, pressing into her and she groaned, eyes half-closing as her hips rose.

Hiding his smile, he slid off of her, palming her thighs through the gown and easing her legs apart. Looping each ankle in the silken bindings, he tied them off at the remaining posts.

Her gown now stretched taut, molding every part of her body to his hungry eyes. But not quite enough.

"I've a special night in store for you, you deceitful little bitch."

"Not fair," she gasped, head lifting to look at him.

"Tsk, tsk. I warned you about silence. A pity you could not obey. You did so well at it while playing my whore."

"This is ridicul-mph."

He cut off her words with another strip of the black silk, tying it behind her head. The fabric darkened further with her vain attempts to push it away with her tongue. Finally, she was well and truly silenced.

"Fair, my lying dove? Was it fair of you to pretend to be something you are not? And to what purpose, I wonder? What sort of manipulation did you have in mind? Blackmail? Marriage? Did you think because you were a virgin, I would wed you?"

God knew it was the honorable thing to do. But he refused to be manipulated and Tori had proved that she was a woman of her own making, her own decisions. If she chose to give him her virginity, then so be it. With ruthless determination, he shoved the niggling doubts to the back of his mind.

Her head thrashed and she twisted in her silken bondage, fingers clenching wildly.

He watched her for a moment then rolled his shoulders, again shoving aside his own sense of guilt. Damn, he could not allow himself to sympathize. His ex-fiancée had taught him well the dangers of sympathy and trust.

Tori mumbled again around the gag and he looked down at her, temptingly subdued. "It matters not, little dove, tonight you will discover the dangers of meddling in affairs that do not concern you."

Turning, he picked up his bag and set it between her outstretched legs. "You realize, of course, you must be punished for your infraction." Not looking at her, Matthew opened the bag and pulled out a knife, holding it up to the lamplight.

She whimpered and he frowned at her. "Come now, Victoria, you know me better than that. Or at least, as much as I thought I knew you. I would never harm you ... permanently." He stroked the blade, tapping it with his finger. "It is merely for show. And to rid you of that bothersome gown. Good luck explaining that to your lady's maid."

He laughed softly as her nostrils flared and anger stoked emerald fire in the depths of her eyes. Raw emotion at last. Nothing planned, nothing calculated.

Emptying the bag, he placed several tins, a long feather and a specially sculpted bit of ivory on the night table. Picking up the knife once again, he moved between her legs, kneeling at the edge of the bed. "Remain very, very still," he advised, grabbing hold of the hem of her nightdress and slicing upward until she lay bare before him.

She wore no undergarments, nothing to hide the thatch of dark hair above her pussy or the swell of her breasts. Already her lower lips glistened and her nipples strained upward.

God, he didn't know if he would survive this retribution.

Above all, she must not sense any weakness from him. Matthew tamped his feelings, shunting the unexpected tenderness and thoughts of forgiveness to the furthest part of his brain. She must pay for her betrayal.

"Now, we begin."

Taking his place between her legs again, Matthew picked up one of the small round tins and removed the lid. The pungent aroma of mixed herbs wafted on the night air. Dipping his finger in the paste, he set the tin aside and leaned forward, gently pulling apart the moist lips of her pussy.

The sweet smell of her arousal mingled with the lavender scent she wore and he inhaled deeply. Keeping his eyes locked with hers, Matthew firmed the tip of his tongue and flicked it rapidly over her swollen clitoris.

Tori bucked beneath him, a low moan escaping the gag. Her hips rotated and the muscles of her thighs clenched in useless spasms as she tried to close her legs.

Settling between her widely spread thighs, he blew on her clit, dabbing the unguent onto the ruby-red nerve endings.

He waited, fingers tripping up and down the sides of her pussy, causing shiver after shiver to wrack her. She smelled of sex and desire, which shot straight to his cock, making him harder if that was possible. He shifted on the bed, not allowing her to see his desire.

"Did you know," he said conversationally, "that sultans of old kept their women in constant states of arousal?"

Her hips danced, slowly at first, then gaining momentum as the paste he applied began its work in earnest. The minor-warming lotion would send her body higher and higher, but without relief. Spreading her lips wider, he blew across her clit, slapping her outstretched thighs when her shriek grew loud, even with the gag.

"You begin to see, do you not? You are helpless against the powers of the paste. I have applied just a tiny bit because you were already so wet." That was the bloody truth. He'd never had a woman so ready to receive him. To his chagrin, Matthew fought his slipping control.

He swallowed hard, reminding himself of her betrayal.

"Mpphw."

Despite the thin gag, he could make out his name on her lips.

"Not one more sound until I give you permission, Victoria."

Her eyes flashed angrily just before she closed them and nodded.

"Good. There is but one more command you must obey."

Her lashes fluttered up and she met his gaze, one brow quirked in obvious question.

"You may not come without permission."

Sweeping his thumbs back down to her soaking nether lips, Matthew lowered his mouth, hiding his grin.

Permission he did not intend to grant.

She bucked and grunted, displeasure obvious in her tone.

Good.

Flattening his tongue, Matthew fitted it to her crevice, wiggling the tip into her drenched hole. Her sweetness exploded over him and he was unable to contain his own moan. Honey slick and twice as inviting, her musky taste was addictive. Matthew redoubled his efforts, tickling her clit, pulling her juices into his tongue with pleasure and ease.

She jerked and gasped with such ferocity he raised his eyes then lifted his mouth away, eyeing her questioningly.

"Like that, do you? Which part, little liar? The potion?" He blew along her straining clit and her lashes dropped, but she shook her head.

"No? As I recall, you quite enjoyed the feel of my tongue last time." Suiting words to action, he lapped again at her wide-open cunny, finding her twice as delicious as before.

Looking up again, he lifted a brow. "Does that please you, then?"

She nodded slightly, before thrashing her head wildly side to side.

Matthew frowned. "Out with it, Tori, what do you want?"

Unfair of him, he knew, since she could not speak past the gag, but it was all part of his fun.

She moaned and widened her eyes looking first at him, then her pussy and back to him, moaning low in her throat.

Understanding dawned and he started, unwillingly impressed by her natural sensuality. And her unabashed mute request.

Curse her. How was it possible this creature raised in innocence seemed to be his match in both sexual appetite and inclination? Why her?

Matthew shoved aside the fledgling idea of releasing her from her bondage, determined to prove to both of them she was nothing more than an orifice, a vessel to be used for his satisfaction.

Nothing more.

There could never be anything more. Even if – when? – his honor compelled him into offering for her, they would not share a bed again. She was too dangerous. He would never again be vulnerable to a woman. Not even to this woman.

Setting his mind back to his task, Matthew lowered himself again, stroking her clit with his tongue, sweeping the openness of her lower lips until she rocked and swayed. He fitted his mouth over her clitoris, tapping the sensitive nub with his tongue, swiping the last bit of the cinnamon-tinged paste along it. Holding her wide-eyed gaze with his eyes, he drew a deep breath and began to hum. Slowly, but with deep, vibrant sound. She groaned around the gag and her breathing grew more ragged, legs and hips stiffening beneath his hands.

Knowing she was on the edge, Matthew intensified the humming, focusing all his attention on her clit, keeping a careful watch on her face.

When her eyes glazed and her mouth clenched tightly over the gag, he withdrew.

Her head dropped back and she grunted in obvious dismay.

Matthew drew to a kneeling position and tipped his head. "Look at me," he commanded.

Her lashes were shut tight and did not budge. Much like a few nights earlier, she was pushing him.

She would not win.

Rolling from the bed, he stalked to her side, reached out and gripped her turgid nipples, squeezing with just enough pressure to force her eyes open.

"Do you begin to understand, Victoria? Do you see how this night will proceed?"

He let go of her nipples, picked up the feather and swept it over the mounds of her breasts, along her sides, back up her arms. She twisted and mewled, promising him retribution with the spitting fury of her eyes.

Moving to her breasts once more, he stroked the feathered quill again and again over her left nipple. She shrugged and flattened, trying to move away, but he followed, tormenting her to an ultra-sensitive state, then switching to her other nipple and repeating the process.

Her teeth bit at the cloth and suddenly he wanted more. Wanted to hear her begging for the release.

He set the feather aside and leaned close to her ear. "If you scream, I will be out the window and gone before anyone could arrive to assist you. All they would find is you. Naked. Aroused. And tied down. Much more difficult to explain than a torn nightdress, don't you think?"

She growled at him, fingers clawing the air.

Matthew smiled. "I'm glad we understand each other."

He slipped the binding free of her mouth, palm hovering over her lips. Despite his warning, he wasn't entirely sure she wouldn't chance it. Besides, he was nowhere near ready to leave. Not to mention he would never humiliate her like that, despite his deep anger. But she didn't need to know that.

The night hour was still early. They had plenty of time left for retribution.

"You son of a bitch," she hissed quietly. Tears swam in her green eyes and she swallowed hard. "Why are you doing this, Matthew?"

He snorted, dropping the cloth to the floor. "I could ask you the same question, you little Delilah. Imagine my surprise when I discover the whore I bought turned out to be you. How could *you*? You betrayed me. You were a virgin."

Tori buried her eyes in her outstretched arm, unable to look at him. The pain and surprise in his voice were real.

She could not believe he'd gone to these lengths for revenge. The coldness in his face when he first arrived frightened her far more than anything he could physically do to her. It was the emptiness now in his eyes, the haunted tenor to his voice that ravaged her. He deserved an explanation, one she never dreamed she'd have to make. She had to make him understand she didn't give him her virginity for any reason other than her love for him.

Tori gathered her nerve to tell him the true reasons, but before she could speak, another sensation assaulted her.

Matthew had moved between her legs once more and something cold and hard slid against her. She lifted her head trying to see what, but could not.

"At Lizzeth's, when you played the whore, I took liberties with your body that I shall enjoy once more. Pity you shall not."

She winced at his use of the word "whore" but knew his derision was no less than she deserved. Then she heard the rest of his sentence.

"What do you mean, I will not?"

"Quiet." A sharp slap to her inner thigh pulled a hiss from her. Though she was certain he'd taken all necessary precautions to avoid detection – Matthew was nothing if not meticulous in his planning

– she did not wish to alert anyone in the household. Marriage to the Colonel would be the least of her worries were she discovered in this predicament.

She'd known Matthew long enough to understand he meant what he said – he would have no qualms about leaving her trussed up and alone.

Not a risk she was willing to take.

"Pay attention, Victoria. This object," he wiggled it at the entrance of her pussy, "comes from the eastern harems where one man can not satisfy all his wives at one time. But as no other may have her, a substitute was created." Slowly the object pushed inside of her, long, cold and hard.

"Oh God," she whispered. "Matthew, what –"

Another slap, this one closer to her clit. Pleasure swarmed her, making it difficult to concentrate. "I warned you about talking."

The object retreated then returned. Over and over, he repeated the slow movements. Incredibly, her insides quivered and pulled, thickening and throbbing as though it was Matthew's own cock delving into her. She struggled for breath, focusing on the growing need.

"Please, I need to..." She whimpered, biting her lip. "Please, sir, may I?"

"May you what?" Matthew slid beside her, draping his trouser-clad leg over her bare one, pulling her apart even more. His hand sped up, forcing the thing in and out at a rate that matched her fluttering pulse. "Tell me what you want," he whispered low at her ear then pulled back, meeting her gaze. "Tell me."

Without the mask and the anonymity it afforded her, shyness overtook her. She could not say such things to him as herself.

"No," she murmured, looking away.

His strong fingers caught her chin, forcing her eyes back to his. The pulsing between her legs slowed down and she whimpered again.

"Oh please, sir, please."

"Say it." His voice brooked no refusal and he pressed the object very deep inside her, holding it motionless a moment before wiggling it up and down.

The motion pushed her higher. It was as though he'd found a secret spot that drove her every need.

"Say it." More rocking, more pulsing.

Tori was locked by the intensity of both his gaze and the sensations destroying her rationale. "Please, sir, may I come?"

The air around them, smelling richly of her arousal, stilled. Then he grinned. A dark sort of smile that sent tremors of foreboding through her.

"No."

"Ohh," she moaned low. "You are an evil, vile, hateful man."

The makeshift cock resumed its slow, infuriating and unsatisfying pace. "And you are a lying, traitorous bitch. That makes us even."

Tori tried to focus only on the sensations roiling through her, but his words kept intruding.

"Had you known it was me, would you have continued?" she finally gritted out, seeking his face in the shadows, an odd hope kindling.

Matthew's eyes burned and snapped, his cock was hard against her thigh. Try as he might, he could not hide the fact he was affected. Abruptly, his hand stopped. "Don't move."

He pulled away, leaving the now-warmed fake cock lying heavily in her needy pussy. Its presence did nothing more than remind her of what she could not have.

Shifting her pelvis, Tori concentrated hard on clenching her inner muscles. If he would not give it to her, she would take the pleasure herself.

She felt him watching her and it thrilled her even more. A litany of short, sharp breaths escaped her as the orgasm rose in her.

"Yes," she hissed. "So close, oh." Faster, harder she clamped her muscles, each spasm, each release like small sparks of fire in her belly.

The euphoria was nearly upon her when he re-appeared and pulled the object out.

"No, damn you, no."

Breathing heavily, she fought her bonds with renewed vigor, determined to break the fabric and use her own hands to bring about the climax she so desperately needed.

"Stop moving, Victoria."

She ignored him, pulling until the skin of her wrists chafed unbearably. His hands covered the small wounds and he pressed close.

"Stop it," he muttered in her ear. "Do not harm yourself."

"Then let me come, damn you. This is not fair." Her voice broke on the last word, fading into a near-sob.

Matthew's own labored breathing sounded ragged and she sensed the struggle he battled within. His eyes were no longer cold shards, but lit with a desire she felt to her core. He was softening.

"Matthew, please," she begged, moving against him. "You want me, I can feel it."

"Aye, you damn minx, I do want you. Something like this," he ground his hips to hers, proving beyond any hint of doubt he desired her, "you cannot hide."

"Then take me. Like you did before. Make me feel it, Matthew, please."

His head dropped to her shoulder and his lips brushed against her. "I cannot."

"Why?"

"God, Tori, what am I even doing here?"

"Please, Matthew. Listen to me. Now, like then, I am yours to command. But you must allow me to come. This denial is not fair."

Instantly she knew she'd said the wrong thing. His head lifted and she saw his eyes had regained their chilly appearance. His jaw pulsed.

"Fair?" he repeated softly. "And was it fair of you, the one woman I believed would never deceive me, to use me as you did?"

"I only wanted you to love me."

Matthew froze, heart lurching. *Love.* It took him a long moment to recover himself. "Love is the ultimate betrayal. I understand all too well, madame. With the impending doom of marriage upon you, it was a lark you sought. And me you found. Me, you requested."

She inhaled sharply. "You know about that?"

"Aye." Matthew withdrew, loosening the knots at her wrists. "The other whore told me the whole tale." He paused. "What I fail to understand is how you even knew Lizzeth's existed, much less how you got there. Or that I would be there."

Thinking to sway him back to tenderness, especially now that he was busy releasing her ankles, Tori sat up, reaching out to him. "Matthew, if you would but listen?"

He shrugged away from her touch and stood. "No matter, what is done is done. Roll over."

"What?"

"Roll over, Victoria. It is time for your final punishment."

She licked her lips, searching his face. "You don't intend to use the crop? The noise..."

He laughed, though to her the sound held little humor. "Worried about the noise and not the experience. My God, how you have had us all fooled. Especially me. But no more. Your true colors are revealed and I have been proven right. Again. Now turn over."

Tori considered refusing, that the time had come to end his cruel game. But desperation drove her to try once more. Mayhap if she proved her willingness to submit to him, he would forgive her. Mayhap more.

She rolled onto her stomach.

"Spread your legs."

Much like the first night when he used that command on her, she moistened. Despite the turmoil he roused, he easily ruled her body. Whether he accepted the fact or not, she was his.

Tori spread her legs, lifting her arms upward without prompting. He retied her bonds then removed himself from the bed. Before she could question him, he returned. The chilled imprint of a round tin settled in the dip of her lower back.

She heard the lid being twisted off, then the slick touch of his fingers sliding down the cleft of her arse. He circled the small pink hole, pushing gently.

"Matthew?" she asked tensely, shock and only a hint of fear assaulting her.

"That night I touched you here. I promised the next time I would take you there."

He pushed his finger further into her rosebud, eliciting a groan and utter stillness. She looked so vulnerable lying before him, the faint marks of his crop still visible. Matthew swallowed hard.

She had betrayed him.

"No, you cannot." Her voice trembled, but her hips slowly pumped up and down.

True to the nature of all women, she lied once more with her mouth, but spoke truth with her body.

"Yes," he murmured into her hair. "And you will take it. Every inch of my cock will sink into your delectable arse."

"Oh, Matthew." The longing and pleading returned full-force. She was a true wanton.

The realization should have disgusted him. Instead, it tempered his anger and gave rise to tenderness. "I will be careful, Tori, and I promise it will not hurt. All right?"

Much as his pride demanded he move forward with no concern to her feelings, an unnamed part of him forbid it. He watched her face carefully, seeking any sign of fear or repulsion. Despite their current circumstances, Matthew knew he could not, would not force this upon her. His own weakness astounded him.

When she turned her sparkling green eyes upward, he found only desire.

"Yes, sir."

The words were his undoing. Every shred of anger melted with her total submission, his need for revenge gone as if it never existed. Now, in this moment, there was only Tori, his beautiful submissive and the gift of herself. Matthew quickly removed his clothing, no longer willing to subject her to the indignity he'd planned.

Matthew returned to her, leaning down to press soft, gentle kisses to her buttocks, nipping now and again at her firm flesh.

She mumbled and fidgeted, swinging her body to and fro as much as she could. He reached up and grabbed a pillow, sliding it under her belly.

"Matthew, please touch me."

He complied, tilting her hips upward, spreading her body even more. In the flicking candlelight, her lips were deep ruby red and glistening with juices of desire but not completion. Stiffening his tongue, he slid it up and down her slit, stopping every other stroke to tease her stiff clit.

Her sighs of encouragement thrilled him, shooting straight to his cock. Moving upward, he swiped along the soft roundness of her buttocks, then inward, paying special attention to the forbidden area he intended to gently ravage. Her moans increased as did her arousal, proven by the juices flowing freely from her.

"More?" he asked.

"Yes, please, more."

Matthew reapplied the lotion that would both numb her tiny arsehole and ease his entry into her. The heat from their bodies would melt the paste, further enhancing the experience.

Rising to his knees behind her, Matthew dipped his cock into her well-drenched pussy. They both gasped as he sank inside. Christ, she was hot and tight. It almost blew his control.

Tori moaned, wiggling her backside, inner muscles contracting. Unable to resist, he stroked in and out a few times, nearly losing himself in her slick depths and muffled sighs.

Reaching down, Matthew used her juices to wet his fingers before pressing one against her smaller hole. She groaned again as his finger slid inside.

He looked down. "My God, Tori, do you know how erotic you look?" Leaning down, he kissed her shoulder. "Both of your holes are filled with me, do you feel it?" He rotated his finger, pumped his cock slowly.

Her head nestled in the crook of her bound hands and she nodded her head. "Yes, sir," she panted.

Matthew nipped at her neck. "Do you like it?"

"Yes," her body waggled against his. "But," her voice trailed off.

"But what?"

"It's not enough."

The softly whispered words thrilled him and he pushed back into both holes. Tori gasped and bucked beneath him, low sounds of encouragement audible.

Her pussy was wet and hot, eagerly sucking his cock down.

But it wasn't the pleasure he needed tonight.

Gritting his teeth, he pulled back, fully lubricated. Easing open her buttocks, he fitted the head of his cock to her rosebud. "Relax," he whispered, stroking her neck.

"I trust you, Matthew," was her only response.

He fisted the shaft and bore down with slow, even pressure. Beneath him, she whimpered his name and he stilled. "Tori?"

"Don't stop, sir, please. I want this."

The tight ring of her sphincter gripped the head of him as he pushed further inward. A sudden release and he slid easily forward, sinking nearly half his cock into her tight channel.

Tori's back arched and she emitted a low-voiced, passion-laden gasp.

"My God," he breathed, fighting for breath. Tori felt so good, so right clamped around him. Never before. He groaned as his cock throbbed in response to her tight sheath.

Tori stared at him over her shoulder. Need hazed her eyes and her lips were deep red as though she'd been biting them.

Matthew hesitated, ready to stop at her slightest word.

"Yes," she hissed, instead. "Yes, damn you."

Her words sent him reeling. He'd never had a lover so responsive. She was a rare jewel.

"More, sir, please, I need more."

Matthew heeded her pleading request and thrust his hips in until his pelvic bone met the soft flesh of her buttocks.

They both groaned.

He remained still for a long moment, then pulled back only to sink in once more with slow determination.

Tori jerked and wiggled her arse at him, begging him with her body.

He acceded to her unspoken demands and repeated the deliberate motions until sweat beaded his brow.

He could not hold out much longer. His hands gripped her hips, leaving dark marks of ownership. Again and again he tormented them both, filling her ass and withdrawing. Slick, wet heat, tighter than anything he'd ever felt, a million nerve endings all on the edge of lust. He couldn't get enough.

"Please, sir, please," Tori pleaded.

Gritting his teeth and tightening his grip, he sank as far into her as he could. Flattening himself along her sweat-glistened back, he moved her hair aside and nipped at her ear.

"Please, what?"

"Please, sir, may I come?"

Knowing she was that close, hearing her beg for permission with only his cock in her arse, sent him over the edge. He withdrew until only the tip remained in her. Fingers tight at her hips, he inhaled deeply. "Come for me, Tori, come now," he growled, slamming into her tightness one last time, spewing jets of his seed deep into her bowels. Her low howl of completion quickly followed.

Utterly spent, Matthew fell atop her quivering form, his softening cock slipping from her still-grasping body.

He remained atop her for several long, replenishing moments, enjoying the feel of her beneath him, the occasional shiver that wracked her and the soft sounds of apparent approval she made. At last, he knew he could stay no longer and sucking deep breaths into his lungs, he stood and stripped her bonds away.

Smoothing his fingers over her pinkened skin, he lifted her wrist, touching it with a soothing kiss.

"Matthew, that was incredible." Her fingers curled over his, a tremor making her voice quiver.

He looked up, meeting her melting almost shy gaze.

That's when it hit him.

"Oh God, what have I done?"

The shyness catapulted into confusion and she sat up. "My lord?"

With speed borne from the need to depart with haste, he dressed then gathered his utensils, tossing them to the bag, loathe now to touch them. These instruments he'd devised for her torture, for revenge, now served to illustrate what a true cad he was.

From the bed, Tori watched him with quiet grace. No screaming recriminations, no demands for marriage. He swallowed rising self-loathing.

In under two minutes, he shrugged into his coat and tossed her the key to the door.

She caught it with a frown. "Matthew?"

Her soft tone, worried and drained, pierced his furiously moving thoughts and he looked at her. She knelt in the center of the bed, the coverlet clutched between her glorious breasts, the pink of one nipple just peeking out from the coverage.

He looked away, cursing himself for noticing even that. "I must go."

"Go?" she repeated incredulously, spirit stirring.

Shoving the window sash upward, he settled a leg outside and took one final look of her, drinking in her tousled, sensual beauty. He wanted to tell her he'd marry her, ease her mind though she did not seem overly beset about it. But his own doubts and wildly fluctuating emotions held his tongue in check.

Could he truly marry her without ever having her again? Take her to his bed without risking his heart? She tempted him more than any woman ever had.

That worried him more than he cared to admit, even to himself. He stared coolly at her. "There is still the matter of your betrayal, Victoria, but that is a discussion for another night."

Before she could respond, he slipped out the window, disappearing into the night.

Chapter Six

"VICTORIA? VICTORIA, wake up."

The snappish tone of her mother's voice pulled Tori from a deep sleep and she groaned, burrowing her head under the pillow.

"G'way."

"I most certainly will not go away, young lady, and you will not spend another moment in this bed. Now, up, up."

The pillow was yanked unceremoniously away and her bed covers stripped away. Glad she'd replaced the torn nightgown, Tori reached for the covers. "I don't feel well, Mother." Not precisely the truth, though her lower body did ache deliciously.

"Colonel Jameson will be here in less than an hour, Victoria, you must make yourself presentable."

"Mm-hmm." Hang the Colonel, she didn't have to worry about him anymore. Even the prospect of sitting and conversing with him did not dampen her mood. She would not have to marry him, nor after today, would she have to suffer his presence and subtle threats.

Ha, put that in your pipe and smoke it, you old codger.

"Victoria!"

Oh bloody hell, had she spoken out loud?

Tori rolled over relieved her body seemed more adjusted than earlier, and looked at her mother, who stood holding a strip of black satin. Apparently Matthew left it behind in his haste to leave. Victoria's eyes widened before she slammed them shut and gulped.

Remain calm. Look guilty, you are guilty. Act innocent and hopefully she will not press the issue. "Yes, Mother?" she asked.

"Get out of bed. Have you heard nothing I've said? It is too late for a proper bath." She dropped the strip on the writing desk and frowned.

"If Glory had not told me you were still sleeping, I fear what would have happened. What sort of impression is that to give the Colonel?"

Tori rolled her eyes, but gingerly slid from the bed. "Don't worry, Mother, everything will be all right. I promise."

The words sounded delicious on her tongue and the promise of them even sweeter.

Something in her tone must have pleased her mother as the frown turned into a smile of satisfaction. "Excellent. It is for the best, my dear, I know you will understand once you marry. Times are difficult without securing the proper future. I shall ring for the maid to help you bathe and dress."

Not knowing what sort of evidence her recent night of passion may have left behind, Tori shook her head. "I'll be fine, truly."

Her mother hesitated at the door then sighed. "All right, but do not dawdle."

As soon as the door shut behind her, Tori crossed to the desk and picked up the satin, holding it to her cheek, eyelids drifting shut. Just the touch of the silken fabric next to her skin roused her desire.

Would it always be this way for her with him? Could he command her to such heights without even his physical presence? Tori giggled and wrapped the strip around her wrist, holding it taut.

Yes, he could and always would. The scintillating idea warmed more than just her heart. Pity she had no time to deal with the effects of a good memory. She must prepare herself to deal with what she hoped would soon be a bad memory—the Colonel.

"Hm, I hope Matthew doesn't show up while Jameson is here. He might get the wrong idea."

She laughed again, absolutely giddy by the prospect of her future. Nothing could go wrong for her today.

It took her less than half an hour to wash and dress, her body growing less sore with each movement. Only sitting at certain angles seemed to aggravate her deliciously abused bottom.

Good Lord, even having written and read about the act, the actuality proved to be much more exhilarating. Intoxicating. She wanted to do it again.

Squirming on the horsehair seat in the drawing room, she tried to banish such thoughts until after the Colonel departed.

A quick glance at the mantel clock told her he'd been closeted with her mother and brother for nearly a quarter of an hour. Probably haggling over her bride price.

Not that it was necessary, but they didn't know that.

"Ah, Miss Ashford, so glad to find you smiling and in good spirits this fine day."

Colonel Jameson appeared in the doorway, flanked behind by her family. Ryder glowered and her mother's face held grim determination. A knot twisted Tori's stomach and she rose, the smile fading.

"Is everything well?"

"Aye, my dear, could not be better. Unless we were already wed, that is." He chuckled, his mustache dancing above his lips.

Tori pulled her gaze away from the spectacle of his bristles and looked at Ryder. A deep scowl covered his face. Her apprehension grew.

"Victoria, we need to talk. Come into my study." Ryder reached a hand out to her, but the Colonel intercepted her before she could reach him.

"That is not necessary, my lord, as we've agreed to all the pertinent details."

Ryder pointedly dislodged the man's hand from her arm and she stepped back. "She is my sister, Colonel and until she is no longer in my house, she has my protection."

Gaze bouncing between the two bristling men, Tori swallowed hard. Ryder was a very dangerous man when crossed and much as she wanted him to toss the Colonel out on his ear, she felt the need to soothe the tension.

"It's all right, Ryder, I'll be fine."

They shared a look of sibling understanding. He didn't like it, but he finally accepted it. With a grunt, he swung away, heading for the door. "I'm going out."

Lady Ashford's shoulders dropped and her head lifted. Her obvious relief caused another wrench of discomfort in Tori. What exactly had been said in that meeting?

Damn, she hated being a pawn.

"Victoria, I have some exciting news," her mother started only to fall silent at the wave of the Colonel's hand.

"Please, madame, allow me the pleasure?"

Lady Ashford's hesitant acquiescence further fueled Tori's unease.

"The pleasure of what?" she demanded, not giving a whit if she sounded churlish.

The Colonel eyed her silently, mustache twitching every once in a while. Refusing to be intimidated, Tori matched his stare, going so far as to raise her eyebrow. The mustache bristled more and Jameson snapped his gaze to her mother.

"Lady Ashford, I will take Miss Ashford out for a carriage ride."

Tori clenched the folds of her gown and widened her eyes at her mother. Oddly, her mother refused to meet her gaze, ignored the mute pleading and nodded. "Of course, Colonel."

"But –"

"I will see you upon your return, dear," her mother said. "We will have much to discuss, I am sure."

Tori scrambled, trying to figure out what the deuce to do. She couldn't be absent from the house when Matthew came to offer for her.

"Honestly, Colonel, I appreciate the gesture, but I am feeling a bit off this morning. I had thought it best to retire to my room and rest for a while. Perhaps we could go out tomorrow?" No such thing, but *he* didn't need to know that just yet. Anything to be rid of the odious man and his blustering ego.

"No, Miss Ashford, tomorrow will not do. Now, collect your parasol so that we may be off." Short, to the point and quite obviously expectant of her immediate obedience.

The unease now blew into full alarm. "What is going on, here? I demand you tell me. It is quite obviously my future you plan to discuss. Tell me now."

Lady Ashford made a small noise that sounded like a cross between a groan and a sigh. Tori flicked a glance at her mother, but found only a pale face and anxious, pleading eyes.

"What has been done?"

The Colonel turned to her mother and sketched a brief bow. "Do not worry, Lady Ashford, I expected this reaction. Believe me, when we return, she will be much more receptive. Come, Miss Ashford."

Wrapping his hand tightly around her upper arm, the Colonel quite nearly dragged her from the salon. Tori was horrified, especially that her mother was allowing such a thing to happen.

Suddenly, she felt as if her family had abandoned her. They had given their blessings to the Colonel's offer. She didn't want to believe it of either one, not truly. Well, she was not going to meekly submit to any of their machinations, by God, she would get herself out of this mess.

Yanking her arm away, she smoothed the crushed material of her sleeve and lifted her nose. "No force is necessary, Colonel. A ride in the park would be lovely."

His bushy gray brow rose but he nodded. "I knew you would come 'round, my dear. You always do seem to have these bursts of emotion, quickly followed by your impeccable logic. Your maid can ride behind the carriage."

The door shut behind them and she climbed into the waiting carriage, heart thudding madly like a horse before a race. Whatever happened in Ryder's study, she must find a way to make it *un-happen*.

Save for the clattering of the wheels over the road, the ride to the park was silent. She would wait for him to make the opening gambit. Great care must be taken, of that she was quite certain.

Apparently, only she could save herself from marriage to this man. And she certainly had an ace up her sleeve to prevent it from occurring, though confiding her lack of innocence to him was the very last option she hoped to take.

But if it came to that, she most definitely would.

"Tell me, Miss Ashford, what interests hold you?"

Ah, nice, innocuous conversation to begin. She could do that. "I am quite adept at firearms. I prefer not to hunt, though. Seems dreadfully unfair to the fox."

He chuckled. "Your tender heart is but one of your many delights, Miss Ashford. Where did you learn to shoot?"

Tori hesitated. "A friend taught me."

"Corwin?"

Slowly she turned to look at him, surprised he would make the connection. "Yes."

"Heard much about him. Good man. Good eye."

Tori said nothing, wondering where he was going with this.

"Bit of a rake, though. Especially after he was left at the altar. His fiancée threw him over for a baron, wasn't it? I mean, who could blame the poor girl? How could she have known he would inherit the earldom? Went skirt chasing crazy after that sordid affair, he did. Never stopped, likely never will. " The Colonel studied her hard. "But you know that, of course. Him being a *close* family friend and all. I'm sure you are privy to all sorts of *intimate* details of Corwin's life."

"Corwin is more than just a roué, Colonel, but he keeps his interests very near to his chest. But you are correct that he is a family friend. In some way or another, he has looked out for me, been a sort of protector if you will." There, let him chew on that for a bit. While she would not claim Matthew straight out just yet, she could infer a long-held, unbreakable connection.

"Hm. Miss Ashford, I..." He shifted in his seat to look at her, an abashed expression on his face. "I do hope you will forgive my boldness, but I would only like to say that I, too, can be a protector. My men looked up to me and I ensured their safety every day I commanded them. I could quite easily do the same for you. You would always be safe with me."

"Safe from what, Colonel?"

"From what - or whom - meant you harm or disrespect. I may not hold title, but arrogant as it sounds, I do hold an enormous amount of sway within Society. Rest assured, my dear, that in the unlikely event should anything ever arise that could mar you, I would gladly, unendingly, shield and protect you."

Ha, she did not need his protection.

If she were honest, though she did wonder for just an instant, what he'd do to her blackmailer. Tori fidgeted on the seat as they made their second circle of the park, mulling his audacious comments. Enormous sway from a man she'd never even heard of much less encountered in three Seasons? Doubtful. And his offer of protection, though quite odd, was not required. What was required, however, was an answer. As happened so often before, impatience got the best of her.

"What happened in the study?" she finally said, hearing the snap creeping in her voice.

No reply, but his hand began a rhythmic slap-slap-slap lightly against his thigh.

"Colonel?"

"Ask me politely, as a gentle-bred lady should do."

Mind games seemed to be a favorite of his. "Fine. Will you please tell me what happened in the study?"

"Not quite perfect, but certainly acceptable. You are trainable, which is one of the first things I noticed about you." He smiled warmly, mustache lifting high onto his cheekbones. "Among many of your fine attributes, of course."

"The study?"

He laughed. "And persistent, too. All right then, my dear, since it appears you will continue to bedevil me until I tell you." He stroked his mustache over and over. "You are much like your brother in both your tenacity and your pugnacious nature. He proved a bit more troublesome than I thought – again much like yourself. But, with your mother's help and persuasion, he finally agreed. Albeit with some reluctance."

From the moment he mentioned Ryder an icy vein of desperation slid through her. She did not wish it to be true, but knew there could be no other explanation.

"Agreed to what?" she asked softly.

"Our marriage, my dear. Your brother has not only given permission for us to wed, but also agreed to special license. Next week if I can procure it."

"What?" she shrieked. "I do not believe it. Ryder would never allow such a thing."

The Colonel's countenance grew dark and furious. "You will act accordingly, Miss Ashford. You will be my wife and when that happens, you will learn your place. No matter what it takes."

"I'll not marry you, Colonel. This farce has gone on too long. Take me home, immediately."

"I understand you've had a shock, my dear—"

"I am not and will never be your dear, Colonel. I will not marry you."

He lunged forward, clutching her shoulders, shoving his face close to hers. "You will. And you will obey me. Do not force me to do something you will regret, Victoria."

Struggling to break free, Tori kicked at him, but the folds of her gown made the blows ineffectual. "Release me," she demanded, true fear shaking her. "Colonel, you are hurting me."

His breath came in short sharp gasps and his eyes remained wild and intense. But slowly he seemed to regain control of himself. Sitting back, he let go of her arms and smoothed his fingers over his mustache.

He exhaled slowly. "Regrettable that you forced me into such a display, Victoria, but I trust you understand this is not a silly little game you may play. We will wed next week." He tapped the top of the carriage with his knuckles, staring out the side window. "I will refrain from visiting you until then, so as to avoid any undue speculation. I would not go to this marriage with any scandal over you."

Shocked into silence by both his actions and his words, Tori rubbed her sore upper arms.

"You will find me to be a caring and giving man, Victoria. You will not be unhappy."

"You don't know me at all. How do you know what I will find?" she whispered.

He looked at her, a hooded gaze that held menace and promise. "I know you far better than you are aware. Here we are."

The coach stopped in front of her house and Tori scrambled out the door, without waiting for either man to assist her. She ran into the house, past the butler, tears now streaming down her face. Bursting into Ryder's study, she cursed when she found it empty.

"Where's Lord Ashford?" she demanded.

"He did not say where he was going, Miss Ashford."

Tori drew a deep breath and swiped angrily at the tears. Damned if she would let that monster affect her this way. Neither he, nor any blackmailer would get the best of her. She was made of much sterner stuff.

Not only that, but she had Matthew on her side now. He would know what to do. Dashing off a quick note, she sealed it with wax and straightened up. Hesitating, she tapped the folded paper against her palm. He might be offering for her, but Matthew was still furious with her. She turned back to Ryder's desk for a moment before rushing back to the maid who hovered in the doorway.

"I will be fine, Glory. I am going out."

"What should I tell your mother?"

Tori battled the temptation to tell her to go straight to Hades, along with the Colonel. Why her mother chose this man for her, she did not comprehend. What did the older man say that convinced both Ryder and her mother to agree to such a ridiculous thing?

"Tell her I went out."

"LORD ASHFORD, MY LORD."

Matthew froze momentarily. Had Ryder found out what he'd done? He wouldn't blame him if he called him out right now, hang the law and the seconds.

Ryder brushed past Stires, storming into the study. Slamming himself into the leather chair facing the desk, he raked a hand through his hair.

Matthew braced himself for his best friend's fury.

"Tori is going to marry the Colonel."

Reeling, Matthew reached out hands splaying on the sturdy desktop. "What?" he whispered hoarsely.

Ryder nodded. "He and Mother cornered me this morning. There is something not right with this whole situation, but I'm damned if I can deduce it."

Matthew stood and poured two brandies, struggling with Ryder's stark announcement. And his relief that his friend didn't know what he'd done. Gulping down his brandy, he refilled his glass, still uncertain what he was going to do. Tori's sudden engagement only complicated matters further. He needed time to think, to plan. He swallowed hard.

"So the chit is getting married," he murmured tonelessly. "'Bout time, don't you think? She's been left to run wild for long enough. Three seasons, Ashford. One more and she ran the risk of spinsterhood."

He didn't want to think about Tori, not about her lies, her betrayal, her body. And most especially about her upcoming wedding. Let her marry the bastard. She meant nothing to him.

Liar.

"Devil take it, Corwin, pull your head out of your arse and help me."

"With what?"

"I must find something to discredit the Colonel."

"What for? And if you're so keen on your *darling* little sister not marrying him, just refuse his suit."

"I did, actually. Refuse him. But Mother has some sort of bee in her bonnet about the whole affair and insisted upon it. Very nearly went into hysterics about the whole thing."

That caught his attention. Matthew lowered his glass. "Your mother?" Finally, his brain snapped into line and he really looked at Ryder, who avoided his gaze. "What aren't you telling me?"

"Nothing," Ryder grunted without conviction. "For years she's been content to let Tori do as she pleased, until suddenly this Jameson turns up and I find my little sister betrothed to him."

"Fortune hunter?"

"Doesn't seem so." Ryder frowned, swirling the brandy in his glass. "The man appears well enough off. Mother's insistence is the only reason I agreed to the whole affair. Figured it would give us time to come up with something to use against him."

"Count me out, old boy. What your sister decides to do with her life is none of my concern." The lie was heavy on his lips.

Ryder rounded on him. "Tori decided nothing. I'm asking you to make it your concern, Corwin. I need your resources."

Eyeing his friend warily, Matthew stood. "What resources?"

"Come on, man, I've no time for this. I know you have sources of information that the Polite World is not privy to, holdovers from the war. You must ask them what they know of the Colonel."

"What if she wants to marry him?" Damn, just speaking those words tore at him. Matthew gritted his teeth and glared at Ryder. "Don't assume she's unwilling, Ashford. You may not know your sister as well as you believe."

Ryder sprang up, slamming his hands on the desk. "What the hell are you implying?"

He shrugged. "Not a thing. I say again what she wants to do is up to her. No one can control her." Oh, but that statement was so untrue. Matthew remembered all too well that he could control her with ease. With passion.

"What is going on between you two?" Ryder snapped. "First the dinner party, now this. You've been acting beyond your usual boorishness with her. Why?"

"She means nothing to me, besides being the bratty sister of an old friend."

Ryder contemplated him, then slung back the brandy. "No," he muttered, shaking his head. "There's something more. Blast it, why does everyone have to be so secretive. What has she done to you?"

Matthew chuckled mirthlessly. He lifted his glass. "She is a woman, Ashford, is there anything more that needs to be said?"

Ryder's eyes widened. "Good God, you're in love with her."

The pronouncement hung in the air between them. While his friend gaped at him, Matthew struggled to maintain a calm façade. Love? Impossible. Desire, passion, lust. That was all he felt for Victoria Ashford. "Have you taken complete leave of your senses, man? She is a troublesome little chit."

"Careful, Corwin, the truth is in your protest. When did this happen? *How* did this happen? This is the most damnable thing."

He gritted his teeth. "Listen closely, Ashford, I am not in love with your deceitful sister."

"Deceitful?" Ryder shook his head. "She is not Cecily. Tori could not lie to save her life."

Matthew remained silent, unwilling to refute the words, though he knew them to be false. She may not have lied with ease or even for gain, but she'd done it nonetheless. And so much more.

"Christ, this is completely beyond all comprehension." Ryder stalked away, returned and gave him a disgusted look. "What I am about to tell you must never be repeated, Matthew. To do so would cause irreparable harm to my family. Needless harm."

The hair on Matthew's neck rose and he shifted in his chair. "Of course, you have my word."

"I would trust no one else with this." Ryder gave him a hard look. "Or with my sister." He blew out a sharp, stream of air. "I am not my father's only son."

Matthew's mouth slacked. "What?"

The muscle in Ryder's jaw ticked and his throat worked. "Just after my parents married, my father had an affair. Lincoln Wolffe was the product of that union."

Stunned, Matthew rose. "When was he born?"

"The records show the day after me."

"But you have your doubts?"

Ryder nodded, striding past the desk to look out onto the garden. "Aye. He came to see me, you know. At Eton. We were thirteen."

Matthew remembered that year, and several more, to be ones filled with fun, entitlement and the discovery of women. "Why didn't you tell me?"

His friend's shoulders remained stiff. "I swore my silence to my father."

"What did Wolffe want when he visited you?"

"Just to see me," he said flatly, turning around at last. "Said he was happier being the son of impoverished country gentry than the high-faluting second son of an earl."

"You believed him?"

"At the time I did. But now I'm not so sure." Ryder smiled faintly. "He's a good man, Matthew. He doesn't deserve or need the scandal this would cause."

With a nod, Matthew picked up his quill and began jotting notes. "What changed your mind?"

"The Colonel," Ryder said succinctly. "I just learned this morning he mentioned giving his regards to Mr. Wolffe. Jameson must be using him as leverage against Mother and that's what convinced her to agree to the marriage."

Matthew winced. For half a second he'd managed to forget about the quandary with Tori. He'd delayed conceding to himself he would marry her, but this sudden engagement changed everything. He could not allow another man to have her. His honor would not allow it.

He'd been the one to take her innocence, however unknowingly. He could not send her to another man's bed in such a state. Yes, he'd offer for her, but out of duty and honor. Not love.

And he must do whatever he could to protect her – and her family – from the disaster now looming. Once this dilemma was solved, he would deal with Tori.

"Have you discussed this with your mother?"

"No, she doesn't know I am aware of Wolffe's existence. I intend to keep it that way. I'll not have her any more upset than necessary."

"Commendable as that notion is, it may be unavoidable. Where does Wolffe live?"

Ryder eyed him warily? "Why?"

"If I'm to get your ass out of this mess, then I need all the facts. That includes any information I can dig up on him. I'd like a look at his birth certificate, too. What has made you unsure of his date of birth?"

Tension radiated from his friend and he cracked his knuckles, looking away. "I can think of no other reason the Colonel would be able to use him against us. Mother would be devastated to learn of his existence at any time, but so soon after her marriage? Think of the gossip that even now would torment her. Her life since Father's death has become the social scene. To have her name bandied about would likely destroy her."

It suddenly dawned on Matthew just what sort of third disaster he was dealing with – along with his own sense of honor over taking Tori's virginity and freeing her from her engagement to the Colonel, he realized his friends were facing a familial crisis that was as crucial to them as his brother's death had been to him. Should Lady Ashford remove herself from society, she would likely take Tori with her. And that, he could not allow.

The only thing to do, it seemed, was rid themselves of the Colonel. "I will agree to look into the matter of Jameson for you. And Wolffe?"

"I'll take care of him," Ryder said flatly. "When this is done, I'll pay him a visit. It's long overdue."

Of course. Ryder never doubted his own honor, never failed to do the right thing.

Matthew looked down at the paper, seeing Tori's face as he'd left her early this morning.

She'd been so passionate, so giving. In fact, she gave to him everything dear to her, including her heart, without asking for anything. She'd never requested he marry her, never demanded he do his duty, his honor. "Do not worry, Ryder, I will fix this. All of it."

He rang for Stires.

"Yes, sir?"

Scribbling out a message, Matthew sealed it in an envelope and handed it over. "See to it that Wiggs receives this immediately. Discretion at the highest, Stires."

The man bowed, taking the envelope. "Always, sir."

After he left, Ryder raked a hand through his hair, frown still firmly in place. "Thank you, Matthew. I know Victoria thanks you as well."

An immediate vision of Tori on her knees thanking him with her superb oral skills rose and Matthew shifted in his chair. How was it possible the chit was a virgin? But he knew she was. Or had been, of that he was certain. Her lively spirit always so apparent when they were together informally, shone beautifully through when she'd posed as the courtesan. She'd been the perfect balance of vixen and virgin.

Until he'd taken her.

Shaking his head, he rose. "Wiggs will contact me soon. I'll let you know what he finds when he does."

Once his friend was gone, Matthew paced the study, contemplating his newfound situation.

How could he have not known she was everything he'd ever searched for, ever fantasized about? A tease, a joy, irrepressibly funny and smart as a whip. A caring nature for those less fortunate, a ferocious protectress of her family and friends. His intimate knowledge of her bedroom manner melded with what he knew of her everyday life and he realized if such existed, she could quite possibly be the most perfect woman he'd ever known.

Their marriage would not be a quiet, docile one and that suited him just fine. He rather supposed he ought to ask her brother's permission. Matthew scowled, imagining the gleeful, knowing look on Ryder's face when he presented his case.

He sensed a lifetime of unending taunting and I-told-you-so's from that quarter.

Oh well, he supposed there were worse things.

There was a discreet knock at the study door just before it opened. "A note has arrived for you, my lord."

Matthew frowned. "Wiggs already?"

Stires coughed. "No, sir. Left by a young woman. Seemed in quite a state, if I may say so."

His brows shot up even as he took the note. "Thank you, Stires."

"Certainly."

Tearing open the vellum, he smoothed out the parchment, scanning the words.

Tori, asking him to meet her.

He crumpled the note and tossed it into the fire. *Oh no, little dove, on my terms, not yours.*

"Sir?"

He jumped not realizing the butler had remained. "Yes?"

"She asked I give you this one, should you destroy the other."

Matthew shook his head and suppressed a laugh. Impertinent little chit. He took the second message.

Matthew, quit being obstinate. I need you. Urgently. I may be in danger. No, I'm not over-reacting. I cannot speak of it here. Please come to the bookstore.

"Bloody damn hell, what's she done now?"

Slapping the paper onto his desk, he spun on his heel and shouldered past Stires. "Should Lord Ashford return before I do, keep him here. Ply him with brandy, but do not allow him to leave."

"Of course, sir. And may I say where you will be?"

Matthew pulled on his riding coat and headed for the door. "Tell him I'm rescuing his sister. Again."

Chapter Seven

"MISS ASHFORD," MATTHEW said as he came up behind her.

Tori whirled, relief quite evident in her pale face. He could see that had it not been for the busy pedestrian promenade, she would have flung herself into his arms.

"Lord Sussex." She curtsied, gaze darting left and right. "I am grateful you could come. Did it take just the one note or both?"

"Both," he replied grimly. "Where the devil is your maid?"

She had the decency to blush. "I'm afraid I am alone at the moment."

"Good God, do you truly wish to ruin yourself?"

An unspoken *again* hovered between them. She looked away. "Mayhap it would be the best thing to do." Tori's head tipped and her brows knitted. With a small inhalation, she nodded slowly. "Gracious, my lord, it is a brilliant suggestion."

"Forget it, Miss Ashford. Go inside, last row of shelves to the left. There's a door leading to a small chamber. I will knock twice. Pause, then twice more. Only then, will you open the door." He resisted the urge to curse, furious once more with her.

Except this time, his anger was directed at her blatant disregard for her societal safety. Again. Shunting aside the mocking voice asking when *he* became such a paragon, he glared at her. "Go. Now."

Looking quite put out, Tori finally huffed and entered the bookstore. Matthew strolled away, ducking into the tobacconist shop three doors up. Perusing the aromatic wares, he made his selection and arranged delivery to his townhouse.

All the while knowing she would be more than irked with him for making her wait. There was no other way to do it. Following her in would arouse as much gossip as her walking down the avenue alone may already have done.

At last he made his way back to the bookstore, slipping inside and to the backroom. Rapping on the door, he looked behind him to ensure no one watched, then turned to knock again, finding instead a hopping mad, bewitching green-eyed imp.

Reaching out, she grabbed his coat lapel and yanked him forward. Caught off guard, he stumbled inside, arms automatically curling around her in an attempt to stabilize himself.

She laughed softly. "I thought you'd never ask." Clinging to his shoulders, she pressed a passionate kiss to his lips.

Tori tasted as glorious as he'd fought so hard against remembering. Sweet and luxurious, like a hot brandy spiced for winter.

With a groan, he deepened the kiss, gently parting her lips with his tongue, seeking the further sweetness of her mouth. She permeated every part of his being and he quite enjoyed it.

Matthew broke the kiss only because the need for breath intruded. Settling his forehead to hers, he closed his eyes and tried to regain his composure.

Odd that such a tiny little thing could so easily destroy both his senses and his stability. Quite a hold she had on him, but he was not prepared to admit that aloud. The little chit had plenty of ammunition to use against him, he knew, and a large part of it pressed urgently against his pants, seeking the welcoming cradle of her thighs.

"You are well?" he asked, hand creeping to cover her backside. "No ill-effects from last night?"

"I am marvelous, sir, thank you. Do you know," she said in a voice of wonder, "that was our first real kiss? Besides Hyde Park, I mean. That doesn't count – you were vexed with me."

He blinked and moved backward. "Have you suddenly lost your ability to count, Tori? There have been many more than one."

She gave a low laugh, pressing tightly to him. "No, no, I meant it was a real kiss – just you and I – no games, no blindfolds, nothing but true passion and desire between us."

Games.

Settling his hands to her shoulders, he pushed her gently away, spearing her with an intense frown. "Speaking of games, care to explain why you bribed a whore to take her place in my bed? And for that matter, how?"

Though it was one he had every right to ask, the sheer bluntness of his question made her wince.

"Funny how everything seems to come back to the Colonel, isn't it?"

Matthew moved across the small storeroom and settled an elbow along a shelf, one brow lifted as he waited for her to continue.

"Blast it Matthew, don't look at me like that. I was desperate."

"Is that what you call it?"

He sounded bored, but she saw the muscle pulsing in his jaw and the anger building in his shoulders.

"No, no, no, you're getting it all wrong."

"Enlighten me."

"I'm trying," she snapped with exasperation, "but you keep interrupting me."

He gave her a sharp half-bow. "My apologies. I'll not speak until you're done, shall I?"

"Good, see that you don't." Tori paced the small room, watching the dust her skirts kicked up, trying to find the right words. The ones that would make him understand not enraged.

"It is a bit complicated, but please bear with me. Apparently when Father died, he made Mother a most unusual promise and had Ryder swear to see it done." She peeked at Matthew and found him watching intently. His regard made her shiver and threaten to veer off course.

"Father promised that *she* could pick my husband for me. And only she. No need for Ryder to approve the match, unless she wanted him to."

"Why do you think he would he do that?"

"I don't know, honestly. But I was only nine at the time. For the first two Seasons Mother allowed me to make my own decisions and rejections of suitors." She paused definitely not ready to reveal he was the reason why she turned them all down. Somehow, she didn't think he'd appreciate the sentiment.

Another whirl and small cloud of dust. She clasped her hands behind her back and rocked on her heels. "Then, this year, she began muttering about husbands and weddings and unattain—uh, unattached men. She told me this was the year for my wedding." Tori looked up at him, a grimace on her face. "Even if she had to plan it for me."

"Evidently she meant it."

"Aye. But I did not think her serious about the Colonel. Not until *he* told me the pact was well-made and unbreakable. We are to wed by special license next week." Tori could not stifle her shudder of distaste.

Matthew finally pushed away from the shelving, stalking toward her. He tipped her chin up, his finger as strong and commanding as ever. "Get to the whorehouse, little dove."

The nickname caused a rush between her thighs and Tori groaned, surreptitiously squeezing them together.

"Ah, ah, ah," he reprimanded her. "Talk now, and if you're explanation is satisfactory, then we will see what sort of reward you get. However," he leaned close, his voice dropping to a low growl, "disappoint me and there shall be consequences."

She shivered, not sure which she preferred. Apparently he saw her dilemma, because he reached up and tweaked her nipple through her day dress, then stepped back with a wicked chuckle. "Continue."

"Right," she squeaked out then cleared her throat. "The night we danced, I happened to overhear you and Ryder discussing your plans.

I was not very happy about it and, I well, it was quite a rash decision, I admit, but not truly out of character. Don't you agree? I am a bit impetuous."

"Exceedingly," he said.

Pausing only to offer a small glare, she continued, "And headstrong. God knows you've told me that often enough over the last fifteen years."

"Why did you do it?" The command in his voice made her unable to do anything but answer.

"I was furious that you would be with another woman. Especially a, a, lightskirt."

"A whore."

"Yes."

"Say it."

Tori tightened her mouth and shook her head. "You are supposed to be quiet until I'm finished."

His low chuckle sent shivers straight to her clit. "Come now, little dove, who do you think is really the Master here?"

She licked her lips, but looked away, suddenly shy. No blindfolds, she'd said. Truly just the two of them. It made being submissive to him as her true self seem much more intimate, more powerful.

"Tori? Who?"

"You are, sir," she finally whispered. "Damn you."

He stroked her neck, his thumb tracing her bottom lip. "I am damned, little dove, never doubt it. Finish your story. You must return before your absence is noted."

"I told Glory I was indisposed and asked not to be disturbed. They'll leave me alone for a while longer."

"Clever girl," he said with a slight smile. "But I always knew that."

Her eyes widened. "You did?"

"Finish," he responded.

Somewhat disappointed he wouldn't answer she nodded, amending the facts just slightly. "All right. Fearful of what was going to happen with the Colonel I made the reckless decision that I would not go into my marriage bed without ever having known any sort of passion. Any kind of tenderness."

"And you expected to find that at a whorehouse? Are you mad?"

She glared at him and shook her head. "'Course not, you dolt. I knew where you were. Gold is a powerful door and mouth opener. Once I made my way inside, it was easy as rubbing two pieces together to find you."

"How did you know I would choose you?" He seemed morbidly fascinated by what could have happened.

She preferred not to think about it, but couldn't repress a shudder of post-apprehension. "I didn't think that far ahead. I just *knew*."

"Crazy, ridiculous, idiotic, little chit. My God, think of what could have happened to you!" He spun away and returned to the shelf, keeping his back to her. Tension threaded his shoulders into stiffness and his fingers slapped against this thigh.

He was very angry. With good reason. "But that's all in the past, Matthew."

He spun around. "You *knew?*" he spat. "What in the blazes could you have possibly known? You were a virgin, an innocent. Did you even think of the position you put me in? You know nothing of what happens between a man and woman in the bedroom, much less the games indulged in by those who frequent a whorehouse such as Lizzeth's."

Stung by his criticism, she lifted her chin. "I've read *The Opal Chronicles*, Matthew, I knew very well what I was getting into."

He snorted. "Unbelievable. This gets more fantastical by the moment. Stories in an elicit paper do not offer a realistic view of sex." Shoving his fingers through his hair, he exhaled sharply and glared at her for the hundredth time of the conversation. "Is that your entire explanation? That you worried about not finding passion with the Colonel rutting between your legs?"

Tori gasped then flew at him. "How dare you talk to me that way? I didn't do it on a lark, you great oaf, I did it because I'm in love with you. Why else would I dare such a thing?" Infuriated, she reached out to strike him, but he caught her wrists in a tight grip.

"You love me?"

Tori looked over his shoulder, refusing to say anything more.

He gave her a little shake, unable to reconcile the wildcat in his arms with the submissive miss of his fantasies. Both had the power to raise his ardor equally. "Answer me."

"Why else would I do it, Matthew? Despite what you seem to think, I am not a whore. I did it out of love. I could not go to another man without ever knowing your touch."

Sane thought flew from him and Matthew crushed her to him, capturing her mouth in a demanding, exhilarating kiss. Feverishly, he worked at the stays of her gown, stripping her bodice down, then her chemise until her beautiful high tits were exposed to him.

Thrusting his hips into hers, he walked her backward until her bottom nudged the wall. With one hand, he lifted her arms over her head, still firmly clasped at the wrist.

"Keep them there," he ordered, letting go only when she nodded, wide-eyed and flushed. Her tongue swiped along her bottom lip and he groaned again.

Matthew caught each of her nipples between his thumb and forefinger, tweaking with slight pressure that grew stronger as her need rose visibly. Her hips swayed and thrust towards him, but her hands stayed in place.

He continued the pressure for a few moments more before dropping one hand to pull her skirts up, making her pussy clearly visible to his hungry gaze. "You're wet already, aren't you, little dove? If I put my finger inside your tightness, you'll coat it with your sweet juices."

Eyes squeezed shut, she nodded sharply.

"God," he muttered before putting words into action.

They both gasped low when his finger slid into her cunny. Tori's back arched, thrusting her tits out further when he added a second finger.

"You feel incredible, little dove. So slick and inviting. Shall I put my cock inside you? Do you want that?"

Again she nodded.

He chuckled. "Not quite that easy, tell me what you want."

Her eyes flew open. "What?" she gasped.

"Tell me. Give me the words. As you, Victoria. Tell me what you want me to do to you."

Her cheeks brightened even more as embarrassment battled need. "Please, don't make me."

Matthew withdrew his fingers then slowly plunged them in, widening them just a bit. Her whole body responded and her arms dropped momentarily before she flattened them against the wall again.

Aye, she was well and truly his. The knowledge stunned and excited him beyond all measure. With quick movements, he undid his pants and shoved them to his knees. His cock, hard and eager, sprung upward and he laid the hot length along her thigh.

"Oh God, yes," she breathed.

"Tell me."

She sucked in deep, sharp breaths then met his gaze square on. "Please, sir, put your cock in me and fuck ... oh!"

As soon as she uttered the word sir, he was lost. Matthew pulled his fingers out and fitted the head of his cock to her tight hole and sank in, effectively cutting off her ability to speak. Her hands dropped to his shoulder, but he didn't reprimand her.

Mentally, he added one more punishment to her tally, but a punishment he would have at his leisure.

"Fast, sir, please. Fast and hard."

Matthew groaned and slammed into her, her back thudding against the wall with each thrust. She took everything he gave and offered just as much heat and passion in return. Her pussy clenched around him, demanding satisfaction as well.

Tori's breathing sped up, coming in little hitching gasps. When her fingertips dug into his shoulders and she ground her clit to him and stayed there, he knew she was close to coming.

"Ask," he panted out. "Ask me for it."

"Please. Sir. May. I. Come." Each word was ground out as she struggled to obey.

"Aye, come for me, little dove."

And she did, spending with clutching need over his cock. The strength of her orgasm triggered his own and Matthew slammed into her one last time, sending his seed deep inside her body with powerful jets.

He held her up for a few moments longer, while they both regained their breath and composure. Finally, he slid from her and tucked his now limp cock inside his pants, then straightened her clothing.

She gave him a weak chuckle. "Will it always be this way?"

Matthew smoothed her hair from her face and kissed her tenderly, accepting the fact he was well and truly caught by this innocent vixen. He would not let her go.

"If it is, I'll die an early death."

She smacked his arm and laughed. "Don't say things like that."

"Come along, Tori, we've got much to get resolved. Any further secrets you care to divulge?"

Tori's fingers stumbled over her bodice, the movement so small he would have given it no heed, save for the odd flush now mounting her cheeks.

"Victoria?"

"I should get home."

"You should tell me what has you so stirred now." His gaze dropped to her stomach. "You're not breeding are you?"

She rolled her eyes. "It is a bit early to know that. But would it truly be such a horrid thought? I rather adore the idea of giving you a son."

A son. Matthew's breath caught and he struggled against a smile. He, too, found the idea enchanting. "We'll discuss that later, little one. For now, tell me quick what other tidbits ramble in that head of yours. I've no desire to find them outed on our wedding day. Or before."

Her fingers twisted one over the other, the pace increasing until she finally tossed her hands up. "Fine then, Lord Inquisitor, I shall tell you. But know it is no harm, no foul. Naught shall be discovered, I promise. I hope."

Matthew's jaw clenched. He did not like where this was going. "Victoria."

Sighing mightily, she peeked up at him. "I must confess I do a bit more than read *The Opal*, sir, I write in them as well."

"Good God," was all he could mutter.

"I'll have you know, I'm quite good." She folded her arms over her chest, lower lip jutting out in a pout that should have looked ridiculous, but instead had him wanting to soothe her injured feelings.

He rubbed her arms and pressed a small kiss to the crown of her head. "'Course you are, Tori. Ah, it's something we will discuss later. How in the hell did you get involved—, no, later. But for now, no more writing or anything out of the norm until we are wed, all right?"

"I can't," she muttered pulling back, worry clear on her face. "I've a deadline tomorrow I must meet."

"Out of the question."

"No, really, it will be perfect. I'll send him one final piece to finish my contract."

"You have a contract?" he repeated, utterly stupefied. Was he hallucinating the whole episode? Must be, it was the only logical explanation really. Why else would he discover he loved this hoyden, have sex with her in a public storeroom, and learn she was a writer of titillating stories in a paper he frequented?

"Under what name do you write?" he asked in horrified fascination.

"Master D," she said in a small voice. "I chose to write behind a man's name for obvious enough reasons. However, I will write this final installment, then hang my nib and quill up for good, all right?"

He knew the name, had enjoyed the stories. Thoroughly and fantasizing about Tori all the while. Matthew raked his hand through his hair. "Let us not be hasty." He drew his finger along her collarbone down to the tip of her quivering breast. "You shall write them only for me."

"For you? But..."

"Yes," he smiled. "Like a sensual Arabian Nights. For my pleasure and at my command."

She nodded, eyes gleaming. "I like the sound of that. Oh, yes," she clapped her hands. "I have a wonderful idea already. I could...mph."

Matthew pressed his palm over her lips and raised his eyes heavenward seeking divine guidance. "One thing at a time, Tori." He swept his gaze over her. "Come, we must depart."

Once he determined they were both presentable, they slipped undetected from the storeroom. Even knowing he was going to marry his dove, Matthew did not wish her reputation to come to any harm. Stopping her from leaving the relative safety of the bookshelves, he studied her appearance once more.

"All right, you look well enough. Return home, quickly as you can. I'll come by tonight and make my offer to your brother."

Instantly tears filled her eyes. "You will? You'll marry me?"

Matthew nodded, incredulous himself. "I will not dishonor either of us by allowing you to marry anyone else. It is a good match."

While it wasn't a passionate declaration of love, Tori heard the words anyway. With a low squeal, she flung her arms around him and kissed him. "I love you, Matthew."

He pushed her away with a gentle reprimand. "Wait until the time is right, Miss Ashford. Propriety, remember? Now, go. I'll see you tonight."

Beaming with pleasure, she winked, curtsied and whirled, practically skipping down the aisles. Matthew's low voice reached her just as she neared the end of the shelves.

"Propriety."

She slowed her steps and turned the corner, looking back one last time for a glimpse of his face.

"Here, now, watch it!"

"Oh, I'm terribly sorry." Tori whipped her attention to the huge, bald man in front of her. A load of books sprawled over the floor, his green felt bowler slightly crushed beneath them. "Here let me help you."

"No need, Miss Ashford, I can do it, thank you." He seemed to flush and mumble, but kept darting looks at her as he gathered up the books and hat. When at last he had them all, he nodded his gleaming head. "See there? Right as rain, yeah?"

"Yes," she said smiling. The whole world was perfect and she could not begrudge anyone harsh feelings. "I am awfully sorry about knocking your books down. I should have been paying attention. 'Fraid I was, well, preoccupied." She laughed and skirted around him. "Enjoy your reading."

"Oh I will, miss, thank you."

Chapter Eight

1,000 POUNDS OR THE Earl of Sussex dies.

A carriage will be waiting for you at the alley at precisely four o'clock. Do not be late.

Tori dropped the vellum envelope back to the bed, staring at her name drafted in the now horrifyingly-familiar script.

"Oh no," she whispered in sudden panic, "I didn't tell him!" She'd been so swept away by Matthew's passion and promise of marriage, she forgot to mention the blackmailer.

"Damn you," she hissed at her unknown foe. She eyed the mantle clock. Within the quarter hour, it would chime four.

Matthew. Hands shaking, tears welling, Tori dropped to the edge of the bed, the note curling in her fingers. Oh God, please, nothing could happen to him. Who would dare such a thing? Why?

Rocking back and forth on the bed, she whimpered softly, refusing to believe the blackmailer had threatened him. It was beyond any comprehension. It was despicable. He could not die. She refused to let it happen.

The situation must be dealt with.

Sucking in a deep breath, Tori crumpled the repulsive note and tossed it over her shoulder. Fear burned into fury. She stomped back to the wardrobe and pulled out the gun pouch. "Dare to threaten the man I love, will you?"

The very small, discreet, and lethal lady's handgun Ryder presented her last Christmastide was exactly what she needed.

Straightening, she slid the gun from its pouch, loaded it and stuffed it into her reticule. Along with several additional lead bullets to be safe.

Tori yanked on the bell pull, pacing the room until Glory's light knock. Unlocking the door, she mustered a smile for the girl. "I am feeling much better now. In fact, I believe a walk will do me a bit of good."

Glory's mouth hung open, her gaze sweeping the floor. "Miss, what on earth happened here?"

Tori grabbed the maid's shoulders. "Glory, listen to me. I trust you will help me, all right?"

She looked wary. "To do what?"

"I simply wish to dress and be absent from the house without anyone the wiser."

"Crimney, ye can't do that, miss, your mother would have a conniption."

"I'll be no more than an hour, Glory, surely you can keep them away that long?" She squeezed the girl's shoulders. "Please?" she whispered, putting all the desperation she felt into her voice.

Tension whipped between them. "It'll be my job, miss, I can't. I just can't."

The anguish in her voice was real, as was the danger. Should her mother somehow learn of the maid's deception, she would indeed cast her out without a reference. Chewing her bottom lip, Tori thought of and discarded several ideas.

Damn and blast, she had no time for this. Matthew's life was in grave danger and she must put a stop to it.

Matthew.

"Listen to me, Glory. I cannot tell you how I know this, but I guarantee you should something happen here, you will have employment. I will see to it. You have my word."

The girl wavered. "I don't know."

"Please. Nothing will happen, trust me. Please, it is very important. I would not ask this of you otherwise."

A shiver went through the girl, but she nodded. "An hour, miss, promise?"

"Aye," Tori whispered, batting away tears. "You've saved a life this day, Glory. Now, come help me dress. Something light and easy to move in."

Should something untoward happen, she wanted to be ready to dodge and duck. Not that she expected any such thing to occur, blackmailers were notorious cowards and when confronted with both rage and a pistol, they inevitably backed down.

At least, that's what she always read in her novels.

She would use the carriage ride to formulate a secondary plan should the blackmailer prove of sterner stuff. A cold knot of dread circled her heart, but she pushed it away. No time for cowardice here, Matthew's life was at stake.

But she truly hoped the blackmailer was the frail and fearful sort – the kind easily persuaded to leave off by a stern warning and gun metal.

"Right, then," Glory muttered as she tied off the last lace. "I'll tidy up in here. On your way, miss, and quick as rain back in bed with you."

Tori nodded and sprinted down the hall, ducking into a small alcove as she caught the murmur of her mother's voice below. When she passed and the soft click of a door sounded, Tori crept with more stealth down the stairs, back through the curious gazes of the kitchen staff and out the door.

A cold sweat built between her breasts as her heart hammered loud and hard. Her chest hurt from an overset of nerves. She really wasn't this brave, but she had little choice. She must resolve this. Now.

Picking up her skirts, Tori kept to the side of the house, staying in shadow as much as possible. Adventurous she may be, foolish she was not. As before, it would only take one set of prying eyes to call her out, preventing her from facing this scoundrel head-on.

Making the last corner, she saw the promised carriage. It bore a black banner over the door, hiding the crest, she supposed. Biting her lip, she stopped and seriously debated the wisdom of her actions.

Oh why had she not told Matthew of it at the bookstore?

Because she'd been quite distracted both by Matthew's love-making and his proposal. Well, not really a proposal so much as a command.

But she didn't mind. And now was definitely the right time to tell him. He would know much better how to deal with something of this magnitude. What on earth had she been thinking?

Heaving a relieved breath, Tori turned back around, only to be felled by a light blow to the head. She blinked into the shadows, trying to see her attacker, struggling weakly.

The fist hovered above her head once more. "We've unfinished business, Miss Ashford."

"CALM YOURSELF, GLORY, no one is accusing you of anything."

Matthew could tell Ryder's words were falling on deaf ears as the maid continued to sob and wail, her pale face turning an unfortunate shade of beet red.

"If I may?" he asked, stepping forward when his friend gave a disgusted sigh of defeat.

"Glory," he said softly, only to wince as her shrill weeping grew louder still. "Glory!" he snapped and the crying lessened just a bit.

He stood in front of the maid, looking down at her bowed head. "Stand up and face us."

She did.

"Excellent. Tell us exactly what happened when Miss Ashford arrived home." Matthew kept his tone clipped, terse with command.

Her lower lip trembled, but she nodded and recounted the events of the afternoon.

"You let her go out alone?" Lady Ashford shrieked, outrage and fury mottling her face.

Glory shrunk away, the tears spouting once more.

Matthew groaned. "Quiet," he roared. "Everyone, including you, Lady Ashford."

"She is *my* daughter, Corwin –"

"And my fiancée."

All three of them gaped at him then. He waved his hand. "I'll explain later, but suffice it to say I came to offer for her today." He turned back to the maid. "Instead, it seems I shall have to chase her down. Again."

"Irony at its finest," Ryder muttered *sotto voce.*

Matthew chose to ignore him. "Did she say where she was going or why?"

"No sir, just that she'd be an hour. No more." The girl looked beseechingly first at him, then Ryder. "I swear it, my lords."

Matthew tapped his fingers to his thigh. "Did you notice anything out of the ordinary? Anything at all?"

Glory shook her head then stopped. "Well, aye, sir. When I went to her room it was tossed like a barroom after a brawl."

"Charming analogy," Lady Ashford muttered.

"Let me see it," Matthew demanded.

"Absolutely not," she gasped.

"Well, I cleaned it up, sir, so there'd be no trouble. But when she didn't come home..."

"Let's take a look anyway," Ryder suggested, heading for the stairs, leaving his mother sputtering behind him.

Matthew was not far behind him. For all his outlandish behavior and his intimate knowledge of Victoria, he found himself hesitating at the threshold of her private quarters. Invading them did not seem the proper thing to do. At least, not this time. The last time he'd been in this room, he'd been blinded by fury, consumed by passion and appalled by his actions.

This time worry and fear for her safety clouded his mind.

He watched as Ryder rummaged through the wardrobe, leaning slightly to get a better view. When it became apparent he couldn't see a bloody thing from his vantage point, he gave up and stepped inside the room.

Tori's familiar lavender scent immediately surrounded him and his stomach clenched. How could he have not known it was Tori behind the mask?

He would not allow any harm to befall her.

"What are you looking for?" he asked her brother.

"Gun's gone," Ryder grunted, tossing a familiar-looking, torn nightgown to the ground before he turned. In one hand he held a leather satchel, an empty cloth pouch in the other. "Least she's got some protection."

"Oh my God," her mother whispered from the doorway, fanning herself vigorously. "Why would she take a gun with her?"

Matthew combed his fingers through his hair, searching for answers he didn't have. He looked around, remembering how easy it had been to flip the rickety latch on her window. Maybe an intruder had come in that way?

But no, Glory saw her leave. Whatever caused her armed flight happened between the time she returned home and left again.

"Were you with Miss Ashford the entire time after she arrived back home?"

"No, sir, she'd been back at least fifteen minutes afore I came up."

"What is this? Where had she been?" Lady Ashford demanded.

"With me." Matthew turned his back on her censure glare and looked around the room again. The writing desk caught his eye and he strode to it, staring down at the papers littering it.

Letters to friends, invitations, doodled scraps of paper. Naught but the usual assortment one would expect to find on a desk.

"Damn," he muttered viciously, swiping his hand across the top, sending all the pages to the floor.

Silence followed his display and he gritted his teeth, trying to contain his impotent rage.

Where was she? Who had her?

Because he knew someone must. She would not leave him of her own accord.

"I will be downstairs, Ryder. I feel in need of a stout brandy." Lady Ashford turned stiffly and left the room, her footsteps fading down the hall.

Matthew looked at his old friend. "What in the hell is going on?"

"I don't know, damn it, but we must find out."

"Aye."

"Pardon, sir, but I wonder if this might help."

Matthew turned, finding Glory holding out a crumpled bit of vellum. He took it, smoothing the paper out.

"Miss has received three of these in the last few days."

Gut twisting at the words, Matthew cursed low, long and vehemently. He gave the note to Ryder who had much the same reaction.

"Blackmail?" he said, clearly bewildered. "But why? What could she possibly have done? And why threaten you? What in the hell is going on?"

Ryder's anger now ran high and while Matthew could offer a few explanations, any of them would likely have him facing his future brother-in-law at dawn over pistols.

"I know why."

All three turned at the quavering new voice. Laurel Edison occupied the recently vacated doorway. "I know, but I'll only tell you, Lord Sussex."

Matthew tempered his immediate irritation. There was no time for dramatics. Hers or his. "Tori is in grave danger, Miss Edison, please tell us what you know. There will be no recriminations, no accusations."

"I don't know," she said, fingers knitted together on her reticule. "It's so bad."

"Laurel, please, my daughter needs us. All of us. Help us find her."

Matthew gave Lady Ashford an approving nod, noting the paleness of her skin and dark bruising under her eyes. She'd aged five years since they'd learned of Tori's disappearance.

"Oh, Lady Ashford, I am so sorry." Eyes squeezing tight, Laurel began a rambling tale of discovering *The Opal*, the ensuing success of Tori's stories and the resultant blackmail notes. Matthew found himself incredulous, infuriated, proud and amused all at the same time. He had a feeling it was a mix of emotions soon to invade his life for good.

But first, he had to retrieve his naughty sub.

"Two notes, you say?"

"Yes."

He turned to look again at the writing desk, now barren save a few papers that escaped his fury. Walking to them, he knelt down and gathered them up. "She didn't tell you about the latest one, then?"

Laurel shook her head. "Another, my lord?"

"Aye, threatening me."

"Good lord," Laurel gasped. "Though it does make sense why she would accost him alone, sir. She would do anything to protect you."

Matthew lowered his head, fighting back a dark shroud of shame. Had everyone around him known her true feelings but him?

Pushing to his feet, papers in hand, he flicked through them, seeing the words but not really reading them, trying to erase the horrid image of Tori hurt and alone. He shoved them into his pocket and turned back to Laurel and Ryder.

"Where did you meet this messenger?"

"Down the end of the alley behind the kitchens, my lord."

He exchanged a glance with Ryder. "Come, we've a weasel to find."

The boy was easy enough to spot – he tried to run as soon as Laurel called out to him. Fortunately, Matthew had planned for this eventuality and watched in satisfaction as Ryder snagged the ragamuffin by the scruff as he passed by.

"Lemme go." The boy twisted and flailed to no avail.

"All in good time, lad," Matthew murmured as they retreated back into the alley, away from the curious eyes of passers-by.

Ryder released him and set him against the brick wall, one hand on his shoulder to stay him.

"Ain't this rich," the boy sneered. "Gentry 'ittin' up ones what ain't got nothin'."

"All I want is information. Surely you trade in that?"

The young man's eyes sharpened and he pushed at Ryder's hand. "'ere now, why didn't ye say so?"

"I'm saying it now. What do you know of Miss Victoria Ashford?"

The boy chuckled and gave him an almost pitying look that had Matthew biting back a smile. He had gumption, this one.

"Come now, guv'nor, answers aren't free, are they?"

"You little guttersnipe," Ryder muttered, reaching out again.

Matthew stayed his hand, pulling a bag of coins from his vest pocket. He jingled it. "The contents for the information I seek, provided I like it, of course."

"'alf if you don't."

He snorted, but nodded at the audacious beggar's demand. "Tell me."

"She writes for some paper, don't know which one though. Don't 'ave use for 'em meself."

"Who pays her?"

"Mr. Thomas Bailey. 'e's got a fancy place couple streets over from 'ere. Done, then?" The boy held out his hand.

"Not quite. Who's been paying you to read the notes between Miss Ashford and Mr. Bailey?"

The beggar's eyes widened and beneath the grime, his skin took on a pallor not unlike a corpse. He scuttled to the side, evading Ryder's reach. "Don't know."

He licked his lips, gaze darting between the coin-filled pouch in Matthew's hand and the safety of the street just yards away. "Me coin and I'll leave ye be."

Matthew held out the bag, making the youngster come to him to retrieve it. With subtle steps he fell deeper into the alley, the boy following until he stopped suddenly, hands fisting.

"Tell me who. Trust me, you'll be safe."

The boy stiffened, wiping his ragged sleeve across his nose, leaving behind a slightly cleaner swatch of skin. "Not afraid o' 'im."

"Who?" Matthew bit out, patience fraying too thin.

Despite his bravado, the boy couldn't hide a shiver nor the quick longing look at the mouth of the alley.

"Don't know it."

Ryder crowded the small space, an austere frown on his face. "I'm done with games, Matthew, he knows who has my sister. Let's take him to the authorities, they'll get him to talk."

"'ey now," the lad yelped. "No need for that. I don't know 'is name, but I know wot 'e looks like. Kind of carriage he drives."

"He drives? Not rides in?" Matthew quickly asked.

"Nah, 'e's a servant, that one."

"Tell me what he looks like."

"Hm." He stared at him then looked Ryder up and down. "Right 'bout as tall as 'im, but uglier."

"Thank you," Ryder said dryly.

"Bald 'ead and 'e sweats a lot. 'e 'as wrinkles on 'is forehead and 'is neck ain't there. Just 'is 'ead on 'is shoulders. Right funny lookin', too. Always in a green suit."

"What does he do when you give him the notes?"

"Writes 'em down in a little black book, gives me a coin, tips 'is 'at and leaves."

"Is that all?"

"Aye, sir, I swear it." The boy's voice, which til now had remained resolute and quick, suddenly quivered. "Can I go now?"

"Thank you for your help, lad, you've done well." Matthew pressed the bag into the boy's hand and watched him scamper to the alley where he dipped into the crowd, disappearing virtually before Matthew's eyes. The boy had talent going to waste, he was sure of it, and when this mess with Tori was resolved, he'd see to it that was set aright. Wiggs could always use that sort of talent.

"What now? We've no more information than when we started and you are lighter in the purse."

Matthew looked at Ryder, then Laurel. "Let's put Miss Edison and her maid home in a carriage and call on Wiggs. He should have some information for me by now. Mayhap he'll recognize this mysterious figure in green."

"We're wasting time, Corwin," Ryder said a bit later as they walked toward a non-descript tan and white building set amidst a row of ones nearly identical.

"Unavoidable and I like it even less than you."

"He works from here?"

"You sound surprised."

Ryder shrugged. "I guess I thought it would be more... nefarious-looking."

Matthew chuckled. "Wiggs deals in information, not crime."

"Ah."

The door opened before he could knock and a slight young man, clad in impeccable butler's clothing, waved them in. "Mr. Wiggs has been expecting you, my lord. He is most anxious to impart his findings. This way."

Heading through the white-washed hallway, they were led into a large room crammed full of books, chairs, tables and one massive desk. Behind it sat a thin little man with a wisp of a mustache, round spectacles perched on his head and a suit coat that looked two sizes too big.

"Mr. Wiggs, you have what I asked for?"

"Yes, my lord, and it is most troubling. Your Colonel is not the most stable of men, nor is he the kindest. His tastes run to the foul rather than exotic."

Matthew's throat clenched and his mouth went dry. "Foul? What mean you?"

"From what I've been able to gather, he hurt two girls quite badly while in India. When a third was suspected, he was returned to England and decommissioned, with full pension."

"I don't understand," Ryder said. "Did he kill them?"

Matthew shook his head slightly letting Wiggs know not to elaborate on the torture he suspected the Colonel inflicted. He did not need to worry over Ryder's state of mind while concentrating on rescuing Tori.

"I'm afraid it's not quite clear sir. Only thing I can tell you for certain is that he returned to England under a cloud, accompanied by his valet and retired to a quiet, crumbling family estate just north of London."

"Do you know where he is now?"

"No, my man lost him. Astounding as it may sound, I believe his valet – a hulking man in a hideous green suit – made my watcher. Despite his brutish appearance, the valet was smart enough to get the Colonel out of the way without alerting my man he'd been outed."

"Did you say a green suit?" Matthew asked, leaning on the desk.

"Yes, my lord. Is it important?"

Hundreds of thoughts and emotions spun through Matthew and he struggled to contain them all, to find one clear moment of logic so he could concentrate.

The Colonel.

"Aye," he bit out. "Give me the direction of that manor, Wiggs, that bastard has my fiancée."

Chapter Nine

IT WAS THE REPETITIVE flick upon her thigh that woke Tori. Reaching down to brush the annoyance away, she gasped when her arms, trapped above her head, did not move. Opening her eyes, she stared up at the rusted manacles clamped around her wrists, the chain joined, pulling her arms up where the metal fastened to the wall.

"Oh my God," she breathed, memory rushing back.

The flick came down upon her leg again and she jerked her gaze down, taking in her near state of undress – only her chemise remained, the matching leg shackles around her ankles and the menacing leather crop attacking her leg in one fell swoop.

"Ah, awake at last. Must say I was becoming dreadfully bored with your fainting fit. Lasted bit longer than I'd imagined. Always thought you were made of sterner stuff, but that no longer matters, does it?"

Tori stared wide-eyed at her captor, his long-winded, nearly cheerful speech sounding more than odd to her ears. As always, his mustache jumped and wiggled, but even more so with his glassy-eyed enthusiasm.

"Colonel," she said carefully. "Where am I? Why am I bound?"

"Oho, you little temptress, as if you did not know." He tapped the whip against his palm, grinning as the echo of leather on flesh died away. "Do not fear, Miss Ashford, we are at my humble estate. Soon to be our estate, of course. And this," he gestured around the dank, stone room. "This is the spot where I shall re-educate you. Rehabilitate you, so to speak."

Her fear eclipsed her surprise with one breath. "What do you mean?"

The Colonel slid his hand up and down the shaft of the crop as though stroking his own flesh. She shuddered in repulsion.

"It has come to my attention, Miss Ashford, that among your few bad habits, you made the unfortunate mistake of becoming intimate with Lord Sussex. As your fiancé, it is my duty to take steps to rectify the situation. So, from this moment, you may consider your training started. There are rules, of course, which you will be expected to obey. Punishment will be severe." He chuckled, a dark, maniacal sound that rolled her stomach. "Very severe and I *will* take great pleasure in administering it. You've been a naughty, naughty girl. I tried to warn you, I did. Tried to help you see reason. Almost had you that day in Hyde Park, but *he* showed up and you fell into his arms like the whore you are. Must be dealt with, mustn't it?" Spittle formed at the corners of his mouth as he said the words with glee.

Tori could hardly breathe, let alone comprehend his vile words. She could see the madness in his eyes.

"Hyde Park? What do you know of that?"

"50 pounds, nay 100. Such a paltry sum for your talents, don't you think? And you are talented, my dear. In fact, I plan to have you write even more stories, but not for that rag *The Opal*. Just for me. You shall recount the days of your training and your pleasure in my service."

Understanding dawned much too late. "You? You were behind the blackmail letters? Swine, I should have known. Only a coward uses blackmail to get what he wants."

The Colonel slapped the crop along her upper thigh and she yelped trying to roll away from the blows, but of course could not.

"Watch your tongue," he hissed before his face cleared and he tipped his head. "Though I daresay, your fair skin is going to look delicious striped in red, my dear. Yes, to answer your question, it was I."

"But why?" she asked, surreptitiously twisting her hands back and forth.

"Tsk, tsk, do not bother, you'll not escape those bonds until I release you." He held up an equally rusted key.

Tori rolled her eyes and huffed out a disgusted breath before she could stop herself.

Instead of retribution, the Colonel merely chuckled. "One of the many qualities I admire about you, Victoria, is your spirit and *joie de vivre*. Always willing to take on a challenge in your usual feisty way. But you will lose this one, I assure you."

He paced the small stone chamber, walking back and forth along the bed, occasionally reaching out to thwack her with the crop. Each time she forced herself to remain still. She would not give him the satisfaction of a reaction.

He soon noticed. Putting his fisted hands on his hips, he frowned down at her like a petulant toddler. "What is amiss, Victoria? I am quite intimate with your desires and the things that please you. Here you are, bound, helpless, your skin caressed with my crop. And yet, nothing. You lie there like a lump of fish eggs on toast." His voice rose with each accusation, breaking on the last word.

Tori swallowed hard, knowing her only chance was to get him to release her.

"How do you know these things? How did you know about *The Opal Chronicles*?"

Jameson shrugged. "My man has been watching you for quite some time. Once we'd established your habits, it was actually very simple to coax the information from the messenger boy."

"You didn't hurt him, did you?"

The Colonel glowered. "'Course not, I'm no monster!"

"Debatable," she muttered under her breath.

Apparently he did not hear as he continued to outline the brilliance of his plan, detailing how he used coin to gain access to the notes, the careful surveillance, the way he primed her mother to accept his suit.

"What exactly did you say to convince her you were suitable? Indeed, to the exclusion of all others?"

The crop tapped a little faster in his hand and he chuckled. "Let us say yours is not the only secret in your family."

Tori jerked up. "What do you mean?" she asked, trying to keep him talking, still fretting with her bonds. Despair rose, but she pushed it away. She must be strong for herself, for Matthew, for their future. "What secret?"

"Couldn't hurt to tell you now, I suppose. You've a second brother."

Tori felt her eyes nearly pop from her head. He *was* insane. "Another brother?" she murmured.

"Mm-hmm. Younger than the earl, but close enough in age that eyebrows would have been raised, tongues set to wagging." The Colonel gave another low, mad-tinged chuckle. "Your mother knew about your father's mistresses, but not about Mr. Wolffe. Took one look at his birth record and turned ghost white."

Tori shook her head. "So what? First born or second, he's still a bastard. Ryder's title is secure."

The Colonel's mustache and brows twitched a rapid tattoo. "Your mother's abhorrence of scandal played nicely into my hand as did your impending spinsterhood. She wishes to see you settled comfortably, which I can provide. I merely pointed out that the whisper of a by-blow could diminish your prospects."

"Ridiculous."

"Obviously not to your mother. She agreed to my suit, but said she wouldn't force you to wed. Knowing what I did of your tastes, I was prepared to offer my own enticements." He tossed her a frown. "Truth be told, I had no idea you were going to be so damnably stubborn about the whole affair, though."

"Then you didn't know as much about me as you thought. I'll never marry you," she spat.

The Colonel regarded her solemnly, the only sound the swish of his crop. "I do not wish you to be unhappy, Victoria. I assured her of my deep love and regard for you. That you would be well taken care of that there is nothing for you to fear from our union. And there is not. You will serve me and I will give you anything you desire."

Tori shuddered. "Damn your soul, you shall rot in hell." A sob choked her and she turned her head away from him, drawing deep breaths.

The Colonel did not respond, but she could feel him staring at her. Assessing her.

"Where are my clothes?" she finally asked.

"Look at me and I will tell you."

Exhaling sharply, she turned back to him. "Where?"

That odd, bright gleam was back in his eye. "I believe you've misunderstood the situation, my dear. You are not a prisoner, but rather a pupil. A young lady in need of instruction that only I can provide. Once you've successfully learned your place, we will emerge and be wed as is proper. The length of time we reside here is up to you. Learn quickly, leave quickly. Your absence will be noted of course, but a few days, mayhap a fortnight could easily be explained away. Especially with your mother corroborating any story I choose to spin."

His madness was well and truly complete. "What if I do not wish to learn?"

The Colonel blinked several times, brows furrowed as though trying to understand the meaning behind her simple question. "Impossible. No, you are the perfect one. I've known it for some time."

She fell quiet, nearly at wits end as to how to get him to release her. "What does this learning entail?"

He brightened. "How to serve me properly, of course. Attitude, language, availability, discipline."

"Will I always be chained? I must say, Colonel, I am frightfully uncomfortable."

"Would you like me to release you?"

Biting back the sharp, sarcastic retort that sprang to her lips, Tori nodded instead.

"Ask me as a good girl should."

What had once been a pleasurable game, a fantasy diversion to be enjoyed only with Matthew and her imagination took on an unpleasant taste. Saying such things to anyone but Matthew made her want to rebel. Her survival instinct, though, cautioned against such defiance.

"Please release me."

"Sir," he prompted.

Her chest tightened and her throat closed in protest, but Tori knew obedience now would ensure her safety later. Closing her eyes, she pictured Matthew in front of her. "Please release me, sir."

His hand stroked her cheek, tangling just a bit in her hair, tugging lightly. "There now, that was not so difficult, was it?"

Tori mumbled in agreement and breathed a sigh of relief when the chain above her head clinked and loosened as he unlocked the shackles. While he moved to her ankles, she rubbed the raw flesh of her wrists, wincing as blood poured back into her hands with tingling force.

"Better, my dear?"

"Yes, thank you."

He smiled in that mad-benevolent sort of way. "Your clothes are here." He pointed to a low stool in the corner of the room. On the floor next to it lay a bedpan and her bladder clenched. "I shall leave you to dress and avail yourself of the facilities."

She blushed, ducking her head and he laughed again, chucking her beneath the chin. "It is nature's way, my dear, no need for embarrassment. Of course, my man Baxter is not here, I would not subject you to such indecency, so we are on our own for a late supper. I've brought a basket of meats and cheeses. A bit of bread and a bottle of wine, as well."

Tori remained still on the bed, watching him as he talked, fascinated despite her better judgment. He spoke as though this situation were the most normal thing in the world.

"Come, come, up and dressed, my dear. I will return shortly to fetch you for supper. Do not tarry."

With that he, pulled her to her feet, bussed her lightly on the forehead and spun away, unlocking the door with a jaunty whistle. He locked her back in, waved through the small barred window in the door and walked away, the merry tune fading with each step.

Tori shook herself from her stupor, ran to her clothes and found her reticule. Incredibly both the gun and the bullets remained. Despite his weeks of surveillance, it seemed the Colonel had not learned that much about her.

Relieving herself and dressing with as much speed as possible, she returned to the bed, tucked the gun between her shaking palms and waited for the Colonel's return. Over and over in her mind she replayed the lessons spent at Matthew's country estate, the weeks of target shooting, the steps to accuracy she'd honed over the years.

Aye, when the Colonel returned for her, she would be more than ready for him.

HORRIFIC VISIONS FILLED Matthew's mind as he raced toward Jameson's estate. Pushing his horse hard and fast, he muttered a litany of promises and assurances that she be well, unharmed and undefiled by the raving madman who held her prisoner.

Beside him, he heard Ryder's horse straining, grunting with each gallop. Glancing sideways, he caught the fury in his friend, more vicious than any time he'd ever witnessed his anger. He was glad to be on the same side in this battle.

"How much further?" Ryder yelled over the pounding hooves.

"Couple of miles, I think."

Ryder nodded and Matthew leaned lower over the saddle, urging his horse faster. The surrounding countryside was filled with bushes and trees, definitely an area not well-traveled. The dense forestry to his right bespoke privacy and seclusion. The perfect hideaway for a madman.

They rounded a bend.

"Damn!" Ryder shouted, pulling his horse sharply to the right.

"Son of a bitch," Matthew echoed, hurling his horse as far to the left as he could, narrowly missing the coach parked sideways across the road.

"What the devil are you about, you fool?" Matthew shouted as he struggled to turn his mount around.

"Gun!" he heard Ryder yell, then the crack of a shot, followed by a thud.

Leaping from the back of his horse, he ran to the road, finding Ryder sprawled face down in the middle, a huge brute in a green suit grinned malevolently from his perch atop the carriage.

He'd seen him before, in the bookstore when Tori had knocked him over. Matthew didn't believe in coincidences. This was the Colonel's man Baxter, the one who'd been following Tori. He clenched his fists.

Baxter waved the gun. "Care for a taste of the lead, my lord? I've been aching to gut you for quite some time."

Matthew slowly moved toward Ryder, crouching beside him, relieved to find him still breathing. But he needed a doctor.

"I am unarmed," he said to the Colonel's valet, holding up his arms to illustrate.

"Too bad for you." The valet pointed his gun at him and cocked it. "I expected better of you."

"Not man enough for a fair fight, are you?"

The bald man squinted at him for a moment and the barrel of the gun wavered, pointing downward but not long enough for Matthew to make a move.

Finally, the valet shrugged. "Fists, bullet, either one will kill you." Tucking the gun into his pocket, he climbed down the side of the coach with an agility belied by his size. He approached Matthew, gleeful menace in every step.

Stopping a few feet away, he pointed at him. "Don't you want to ditch your fancy clothes, my lord?" he sneered. "Don't want them getting bloodied up, do we?"

"Won't be a problem," Matthew replied, whipping out his own pistol and firing quickly. "I never said I was going to fight fair, either."

Fingers clutching the bleeding hole in his chest, the man fell to his knees. He looked up at Matthew, surprise clear on his face. "Bastard," he muttered and fell to the right.

Matthew relieved him of his gun then turned his attention to Ashford who still lay motionless on the ground. "Ryder?" He turned him over, wincing at the blood spreading across his coat.

Ryder's eyes opened. "Damnation, that hurts."

Breathing a relieved sigh, Matthew pulled back the coat lapel, examining the damage. "It's only a shoulder wound. You'll live."

"Only?" Ryder grumbled, pushing himself to a sitting position with a deep groan. "Christ, that hurts."

"No time for sympathy, Ashford, I've got to find Tori before he harms her."

Ryder gasped again, gaining Matthew's attention. Mayhap the bullet did more damage than he'd thought. "What? Did it hit lower?"

Ryder shook his head, one hand reaching past him. "Tori," he muttered.

Matthew nodded. "Aye, you're right. You'll be fine. I've got to get to her."

"Nay," Ryder muttered, nodding. "There."

Matthew began to worry the fall from the horse damaged his friend's brain. "Aye, she's at Jameson's estate." He spoke slowly. "Will you be all right until I return?"

"I believe, my lord, my brother is trying to tell you I'm right here."

Matthew spun around. "Victoria."

She stood at the head of the coach, hair tumbled down, clothing haphazardly covering her body, slippers in shreds. And a gun clasped tightly in her right hand.

Not trusting what his own eyes told him, he sprang to his feet and raced the short distance to her. "My God, love, are you all right? Are you hurt?" He touched her everywhere, stroking her hair and shoulders, caressing the curve of her back and back up her arms, seeking injuries, grateful to find none.

"Matthew," she said softly, leaning into him.

He took her into his arms, wrapping her tightly to him, vowing never to let her from his sight again. Overwhelmed by emotion, he choked back a sob, pressing his face into her hair, inhaling her lavender essence.

"Tori," he whispered, voice breaking. His body shook and tears formed in his eyes. His heart thudded as though it would spring from his body with the emotions encompassing him.

It was not honor, not duty, not any sense of righting a wrong that compelled him to marry Tori. It was his own heart. The one that stopped beating the minute he'd learned of her abduction. The one that now threatened to burst from his chest as he held her.

In that instant, Matthew knew he loved her, that she could heal him. Had already started. His life had been one of half-truths, deceit and secrets. With Tori, he could be himself without worry. It was a gift beyond all comprehension and she gave it willingly.

"God, Tori, I thought I'd lost you." Unable to stop, his hands still roved her body, seeking pain or discomfort. "Did he hurt you? Are you well?"

The gun fell to the ground as her hands turned soothing, stroking his hair and shoulders, though he felt fine tremors running through her. She pulled back and he resisted. "I'm fine, my lord." Her voice sounded oddly flat, distant.

Alarm rang through him.

"What happened? How did you gain your freedom?" He looked down at her, wincing at the ashen pallor of her skin and the wildness in her eyes. He was so intent on reassuring himself she was safe, he'd not given a thought to her mental state. "Tori," he said soothingly. "Little one, where is the Colonel?"

Her mouth opened and closed, small gasps of air escaping but no sound.

"Breathe slowly, focus, try to recall. It's all right," he murmured. "You are safe now."

Tori's eyes fluttered shut and her nostrils flared as she inhaled, then let it out with force. "Matthew, please, don't think ill of me. I did what I had to do, I swear it. He left me no choice." Her entire body shook, tiny spasms that traveled down and back up.

Matthew gripped her shoulders. "What happened?"

"God forgive me," she sobbed. "I shot him."

Chapter Ten

"WHERE IS SHE?" LADY Ashford's screech could be heard quite clearly all the way to Matthew's study.

Tori, wrapped in a warm blanket, looked at her brother. "We are in agreement? You won't back down?"

Ryder shook his head and stood, facing the doorway. "We are in here, Mother," he called, voice strong.

She burst into the room, her appearance quite a shock to Tori. Rising with concern, she studied the disheveled, nearly unkempt version of her mother. "What is amiss? Are you unwell?"

"Victoria Rose." Her mother drew her name out in long, imperious syllables. "Where have you been? You have quite a lot of explaining..." She trailed off, staring at Tori, a bit of wildness in her eyes. "Oh, hang it all, are you hurt?"

Tori, stunned by the breach of verbal etiquette, was further shocked by the sweeping embrace of her mother. Wrapped in her arms, a place she'd not been since the schoolroom, broke the reserve she'd managed to hold in place since her kidnapping.

Quiet tears, followed by deep hiccups and near-wails, escaped her and Tori buried her face in the crook of her mother's neck, finding unexpected solace.

"Oh Mama," she cried over and over.

Lady Ashford's trembling hands maintained a steady brush up and down her back, along the crown of her head and neck, providing maternal comfort sorely needed.

At last the storm quieted and Tori regretfully pulled away, embarrassed by her lack of control.

"I'm sorry, Mama," she murmured.

"Hush, dear, there is nothing to apologize for. Not from you, at any rate." Lady Ashford's voice broke slightly.

"Why do you ladies not seat yourselves? I will have Stires fetch us more tea and a light supper."

Tori turned to him, smiling through still-damp eyelashes and Matthew's heart clenched. God, he never again wanted to see such desolation, such hurt on her face. He bowed to them. "Please excuse me."

"Of course, my lord," Lady Ashford assented. "But we will speak when you return."

"I look forward to it."

After directing the staff, Matthew took advantage of the time to change clothes and gather himself. It was not every day a man found himself in love and the object of that emotion in danger.

He found little pleasure in lying to her, but her state of mind was more important than any deception he wove. Telling her the Colonel had survived her gunshot, but apparently took his own life, had only served to soothe her frayed nerves. The small white lie—indeed, she'd proven a crack shot -- served its purpose, bringing her out of her ennui. He was content.

Tugging the sleeves of his jacket to crisp ends, he returned to the study, finding the primaries of this odd series of events huddled on the settee and facing the low table. The four of them spoke in hushed, serious tones. He looked quickly at Tori, finding her relaxed though intent on her brother's words.

The conversation continued as he joined them, lifting a startled Tori from the couch and depositing her on his lap.

"Matthew," she reprimanded him, shooting a blush-filled look at her mother.

"Never mind," he replied. "She'll just have to get used to it."

"I will, will I?" Lady Ashford said in her more normal stately tones.

"Aye."

"And what sort of life can you provide for my daughter, Corwin? You are quite the rake. A roué is not what I ever intended for my daughter."

"Mother!" Tori protested.

"Hush," Lady Ashford murmured, though with none of the acidity Matthew had grown accustomed to from her. Mayhap the incident had mellowed her. For Tori's sake, he hoped so.

"I promise I shall treat her as well as any queen has ever been treated." Surreptitiously snaking his hand under Tori's gown, he gave a light pinch to her bum, making her jump ever so slightly. "I shall see to it she wants for naught. I will fill her days with joy and her nights with love." He no longer spoke to her mother or brother, but directly to Tori, his heart in every word.

Stroking her cheek, he leaned forward and pressed a gentle kiss to her brow. "I will give you everything you ask for and so much more. Never shall a day pass that you will not know how deeply I love you."

Tori remained quiet and still on his lap. She raised a trembling hand and swept it over his hair, leaning close to his ear, whispering her scandalous request so only his ears heard it.

"And will you punish me when I deserve it, my dark master?"

Chapter Eleven

"YOU HAVE A VERY SMUG smile on your face, Lady Sussex," Matthew commented much later that evening. He stood behind her, watching as she brushed her long, cocoa-brown hair.

"Lady Sussex. I find the title quite remarkable, my lord."

He took the brush from her hand and laid it on the table. "I find *you* quite remarkable." Matthew slid the collar of her cotton nightdress aside, baring her shoulder. Watching her in the mirror, he leaned down and brushed his lips to her warm flesh.

Her eyelids fluttered as she lolled her head sideways. She cupped his face lightly, urging him to continue. With grateful greed, he suckled her golden skin, delighting in the shiver of her response. How he'd missed touching her.

In the rush of wedding preparations, they'd been unable to do more than snare an occasional secretive kiss and fondle. It had not been enough for either of them.

Matthew growled low in his throat and swooped her up from the chair, carrying her across the room to the bed. Tossing her lightly upon the downy covers, he planted his hands to his hips and playfully scowled at her.

"I've a hunger for you, wench."

Flipping her hair from her eyes, Tori raised up on her elbows. She bent her knee causing her gown to slide up, revealing her tawny thigh. "Is that so?"

"Aye," he muttered, yanking his shirt from his pants, swiftly unbuttoning it, letting it fall to the floor. His boots and stockings soon followed. Hesitating over the fastening of his breeches, he raised a brow. "And what do you want, Tori?"

The air filled with a thickness that left him uneasy. "Tori?"

His new wife bit her lip and looked away from him, staring instead at the fire as though she'd never seen such a thing.

"Victoria," he said sharply.

She jumped then pushed herself to a sitting position. "My lord... Matthew, I, I would like to request a boon. A bridal gift."

Tension knitted her delicate brows together and he caught the rapid rise and fall of her breathing beneath the voluminous nightdress. Whatever boon she wished to request, had her on edge.

"Anything, Tori."

A sharp inhalation, a quick peek up at him, then silence.

Matthew frowned at her. "You must tell me, else I cannot grant it."

"It's a bit embarrassing, my lord," she said, her voice a mere whisper.

"Then we'll not speak of it." He was thoroughly confused now. Though eager to re-acquaint them both with the joys of love-making, he would not rush her.

"Oh, but we must," she blurted out, finally looking up at him.

"Victoria," he gritted out.

"My lord." She gained her feet and closed the distance between them. "My... encounter left me a bit unsettled."

Ah. "It's to be expected, of course."

"Nay," she shook her head. "Let me speak."

He raised a brow and nodded. "Pray do so. Quickly."

"Hmph. I am trying to. Where was I?"

"Unsettled."

"Right. Yes. Well, as to that, it's not really the kidnap, nor the unfortunate result that has me so dismayed, but what occurred in between."

Tori peeked up at her husband -- la, how she loved that word -- and drew a steadying breath. If she was ever to resolve this unexpected side effect of her ordeal, she must draw strength and tell him.

"When I was at his mercy, I found myself to be in quite a similar position as I did *our* first night together."

"Lord, woman, it was nothing alike." He sounded horribly offended.

"No, of course not, and that is the problem, Matthew," she rushed to assert. "I felt nothing save revulsion and true fear while he had me bound."

Oh, please, work it out. Do not make me say it.

Apparently, some unspoken prayers were answered. Matthew's face cleared immediately. "You don't mean?"

"Aye, I do."

"And you wish to discover whether the joy of that bondage is gone forever?"

"Yes, sir," she said automatically, head lowering.

He tipped her face up. "You are sure, Tori? You wish to spend our first night together as man and wife submitting to me? In all ways?"

Unable to stop herself, Tori knelt in front of him, holding his hand and looking up at him. "I pledged my troth to you in front of God and the Ton this morning. Now, I would give you my obedience, if you would have it."

He chuckled, raising her up and wrapping her in his arms, kissing her deeply. "You know, of course, that I am but putty in your hands and *you* truly command *me*? I will never do you harm or treat you as though you are not worthy. You know this, no matter what?"

"Aye, my lord."

The change came over him suddenly, altering him from concerned husband to arrogant master in one subtle shift of his expression. Tori's body reacted instantly, wetting with anticipation, nipples straining toward his touch.

"Come here, little dove and take my cock out from my pants. We shall see if marriage has deprived you of your excellent cock-sucking talents."

Tori scooted across the floor, eagerly reaching for the front of his breeches. Reaching inside the soft linen, she grasped his hardness and pulled it out.

Wetting her lips, she inhaled deeply, loving his musky aroma. His hands fisted in her hair, moving her forward.

Tori opened her mouth wide, engulfing the head of his cock, clamping her lips around it and pulling hard.

He could not squelch his appreciative groan. Matthew's fingers tightened, urging her onward.

Tori sucked as much of his length into her mouth as she could, stalling only when he filled her totally. She gagged when he pushed against the back of her head, forcing her to take more.

"You can do it, dove, relax your throat. A true little whore can deep-throat any man."

The naughty words only inflamed her more and she did as instructed, allowing the muscles in her throat to open wider, grunting as he slid forward. A thin salty trickle escaped his cock head, coating her mouth.

They both groaned.

"Damn you, woman, you're going to make me spend already. Do not do it. You will regret it." His hand pulled again and his hips thrust forward.

Tori could not resist the challenge or the unspoken promise of punishment. Encircling the base of his shaft with her right hand, she continued to suck him deeply into her throat, while cupping his tightening balls with her left. Little pinches and scrapes with her nails, coupled with the suction drove him closer to the edge.

"My God, you are the best cock-sucker." His words, grunted out in rhythm with his thrusting hips, thrilled her.

Throwing all caution to the wind, she left his balls and found the tight, puckered ring of his anus. Pushing gently inward, she inhaled sharply and was rewarded by his shout of completion, followed immediately by the salty splash of his seed as he came in her mouth.

Tori continued to lightly rub with her finger, pulling every drop she could from him, all the while holding her own orgasm back.

When he'd at last been drained, his hands left her hair and she rocked back on her heels, grinning up at him with arrogant delight.

"Enjoyed it, did you?"

His chest heaved and a flush coated his high cheekbones. "Aye, you minx. I believe I told you not to make me come, didn't I?"

Thoroughly enjoying the game again, she attempted a regretful look, knowing she'd failed miserably. "I'm sorry, sir."

Cupping her under the arms, he pulled her up, tugging the nightgown from her head. Quickly, he spun her 'round, forcing her to bend over the bed. "Sorry will not do. It's a proper punishment I've in mind for you. Ten, I believe. Do not move."

Her knees quivered in anticipation and her cunny fairly dripped with delight. She ached and spasmed just at the thought of what he was about to do to her.

What she wanted him to do.

Her hands fisted the bedsheets and she peered over her shoulder, seeking him out. He rummaged in a tall dresser, pulling out a crop.

Tori groaned and he whirled.

"I do not remember giving you permission to look. Another five, it shall cost you."

He moved behind her once more. "Spread your legs."

She complied, inching them apart, resting more weight on her elbows.

The crop tapped her naked bum. "Wider."

Tori spread her feet on the rug-covered floor, squeezing her eyes shut, eagerly awaiting the first blow.

Instead, she felt him lay his body along hers, pressing her closer to the bed. His mouth nipped at her ear. "It's a lifetime of pleasure we've to look forward to, my love."

"Aye, my lord," she sighed, happier than she'd ever been in her life.

"You know I love you."

"Aye. I love you, too, sir." She wriggled her bottom.

His chuckle reverberated along her spine and his fingers slid along her cunt, delving into the wetness. "All right, my impatient little slut. I suspect you'll be sitting quite gingerly for the next few days."

Matthew lifted up again, sliding the crop along the ridge of her spine and to the cleft of her arse. "Count them," he ordered and lifted the whip, bringing it slashing down on her delicate skin.

She moaned and thrust her bottom up higher, looking at him over her shoulder. "One, sir. Of many for years to come."

THE END

Don't miss out!

Visit the website below and you can sign up to receive emails whenever Jennifer August publishes a new book. There's no charge and no obligation.

https://books2read.com/r/B-A-ZISF-IRAMB

About the Author

I've been spinning tales since I was a little tyke. My mom called me crécelle when I was young, which means little noisemaker in French (literal translation is rattle!). I loved making up stories to entertain my family, moving from recaps of my day that included fascinating things like how many crayons I broke at daycare to how fast I could run (not very) on the playground.

As I grew up and found romance novels, I knew without a doubt, this was my passion and my true calling in life. Growing up in a tight-knit family, I knew what true love looked like and I wanted to parlay those feelings into my characters. I love finding crazy situations for my poor characters to navigate through whether it's medieval curses, Regency England treasure hunts, serial killers, or hot menage scenes.

I hope you enjoy my books and I'd love to hear from you! Email me at jenniferaugust@jenniferaugust.com

Read more at https://www.jenniferaugust.com/.

www.ingramcontent.com/pod-product-compliance
Lightning Source LLC
LaVergne TN
LVHW090954080826
845145LV00003B/999
9781940061047